KT-418-014

WELCOME TO
WEIRDSVILLE

Happyland

I. M. Strange

LITTLE, BROWN BOOKS FOR YOUNG READERS
lbkids.co.uk

With special thanks to Jan Gangsei

LITTLE, BROWN BOOKS FOR YOUNG READERS

First published in Great Britain in 2013 by Little, Brown Books for Young Readers

Copyright © 2013 by Working Partners

The moral right of the author has been asserted.

*All characters and events in this publication, other than those
clearly in the public domain, are fictitious and any resemblance
to real persons, living or dead, is purely coincidental.*

All rights reserved.
No part of this publication may be reproduced, stored in a
retrieval system, or transmitted, in any form or by any means, without
the prior permission in writing of the publisher, nor be otherwise circulated
in any form of binding or cover other than that in which it is published
and without a similar condition including this condition
being imposed on the subsequent purchaser.

A CIP catalogue record for this book
is available from the British Library.

ISBN 978-0-349-00125-8

Typeset in Minion by M Rules
Printed and bound in Great Britain by
Clays Ltd, St Ives plc

Papers used by LBYR are from well-managed forests
and other responsible sources.

MIX
Paper from
responsible sources
FSC® C104740

Little, Brown Books for Young Readers
An imprint of
Little, Brown Book Group
100 Victoria Embankment
London EC4Y 0DY

An Hachette UK Company
www.hachette.co.uk

www.lbkids.co.uk

WELCOME TO
WEIRDSVILLE

Happyland

60000241206

WELCOME TO WEIRDSVILLE

Happyland
Ghost School
Dog Eat Dog

For Sven –

Happy 11th birthday, buddy!

Northamptonshire Libraries & Information Service WE	
Askews & Holts	

CHAPTER 1

What a day! The hot sunshine hit the pier and the abandoned amusement park, casting shadows across our football game. It was my birthday. Lucas, Emma and I had this entire stretch of beach to ourselves. Not a cloud in the sky or soul in sight to wreck our fun. Nothing could possibly go wrong.

That's what I thought, anyway.

I dribbled the ball across the sand, sidestepping Emma's attempt to tackle me. In my mind the crowd

was going wild. I imagined the stadium on its feet, chanting: *"To-by! To-by!"*

Lucas yelled from the other side of the beach. "Toby!" He flapped his arms. "To me! On the wing!"

I looked up, pushed my hair out of my face and swung my leg. *Yes!* Straight to his feet.

As usual, Lucas missed.

"Oops," he said, watching the ball roll between his legs. Lucas is my best friend – and probably the cleverest guy I've ever met. He can calculate the square root of eight billion in his head. And he knows the distance from Earth to Mars, to the nearest millimetre. But when it comes to coordination, he's hopeless. Most of the time he walks around with his flies undone and glasses on wonky. Even his hair doesn't look like it knows which direction to go. Up. Down. Sideways.

Emma dodged behind Lucas and took the ball. She dribbled it away, cheering.

"And the defender gets possession!" She shook her arms above her head and danced. Sand flew around her feet.

I laughed. Emma's my next door neighbour, and she might be a girl, but she's actually all right. Good at football, too. She can be a bit of a nutcase though – when we were six, I watched Emma back her dad's Fiat Punto out of her driveway. She used a cricket bat to push the pedals.

A flock of seagulls screeched and circled overhead.

Emma looked up. "Cooooool!" She whipped out her camera phone and began filming two birds having a fight over a mouldy chip.

Like I said . . . a bit of a nutcase.

Lucas took advantage of the distraction and got the

ball. He grinned, aimed at me and smashed it . . . really wide. It skidded across the sand and hit the back of someone's legs, bounced off and rolled to a stop. Unfortunately the legs belonged to the worst person ever to stomp down the corridors of Weirville Comprehensive.

Keira Ramone.

I groaned. Where did she come from? It wasn't enough to be the nightmare of our school year – she had to show up and ruin the summer holidays, too.

Keira turned, saw us and flashed a wicked grin. Her silver braces glinted in the sun. On anyone else, that mouth full of metal would be nerdy. On Keira, it was battle armour.

"Lose something?" She flicked the ball in the air, bounced it off her knee, then caught it on her foot. *Show off.* Keira's a year ahead of me at school, but we're in the same squad. And she's just as big a bully on the field as she is everywhere else.

"Hey! I asked you muppets a question." She flicked the ball up, headed it and caught it with both hands. "This yours, Lucas Pukas?"

One time, two years ago, Lucas had thrown up on a Geography field trip. And Keira was never going to let him forget it.

My best mate shuffled backward, shaking his head. If it weren't for me, Keira would probably stuff Lucas in his locker on a daily basis.

I forced a smile.

"Hey, Keira," I said. "It's mine. Birthday present. Can I have ..."

Keira silenced me with an evil glare.

"Birthday?" she said. "Shouldn't you be off drinking strawberry milk and playing pin the tail on the donkey? Or has Lucas got sick of having pins jabbed in him?" She snorted.

My hands balled into fists. I stuffed them in my pockets.

"Good one," I said. "Come on, Keira. Just kick it over."

Keira shrugged. "If you say so." And with a grimace, she drop-kicked the ball and sent it flying.

My brand new Nike T90 hand-stitched football sailed across the beach, over the tangle of barbed wire and mesh-covered fence that edged the pier, right into the dark depths of the old amusement park.

"No!" I yelled.

Lucas, Emma and I raced to the fence and peered between the chain-links.

A giant sign saying HAPPYLAND – HOME OF HAPPY THE CLOWN! hung crookedly over a row of turnstiles

6

that looked like they'd rusted shut decades ago. The sign wobbled back and forth in the breeze. I reckon the thing used to be colourful. Once. But now, years of salt air and sun had nearly bleached away the red, green and blue letters, and the sketch of Happy's head was no more than a jagged outline.

I looked deeper into the park for any sign of my ball, trying to control the shiver that had begun to creep up my neck.

Beyond the turnstiles, a huge roller coaster rose into the sky, jutting out past the edge of the pier so it was over the sea and twisting behind rows of abandoned stalls. A plastic hedge maze took up a section in the middle. And a faded big top tent poked up in the distance at the end of the pier. All a big, run-down mess.

And my ball was nowhere to be seen.

"Happyland? This place looks about as happy as a cemetery," said Emma.

The fluorescent sign on the fence said: DANGER! – NO UNAUTHORISED ACCESS!

"I'll never get my ball back now," I said.

"Sorry, mate," Lucas said.

I sighed. "It's not your fault."

"Oops! Bad luck, losers," called someone from behind us.

I turned to see Keira standing there, smirking. Why couldn't she just leave us alone? My hands clenched again. One of these days I was really going to let her have it. I started to open my mouth, but just then a cold breeze blew over the fence, making me shudder. A lone seagull squawked and flew away.

Silhouetted against the sky was a balloon, drifting

towards us from out of the park. A black balloon. It sank in front of me and hovered there. Twirling at the end of its string was a small black envelope.

I glanced around, then reached out shakily and grabbed it.

"What the . . . ?" Emma said.

Back inside the park a sudden shock of orange and white caught my eye. A clown. His bright red lips were painted into an artificial smile, and his eyes were made up in mock surprise. He watched us a moment, then waved with an oversized white glove. Every hair on my body stood on end. The clown walked behind a stall and was gone.

"Did you see that?" Lucas raised a shaking finger in the direction of the clown. Emma fidgeted with her camera phone, rapidly pushing buttons and checking the tiny screen.

"Lame! Missed it!" she said, shoving the phone back in her pocket.

I flipped the envelope over in my hand.

The word Toby was scrawled across the front in blood-red pen.

I gulped and thought about chucking the thing back over the fence. But before I could, Keira yanked it from my hands. "Let me see!" she said.

She ripped open the envelope. A black card with a white 11 on the front slid out, and four identical black slips of paper fluttered to the ground. I picked them up:

```
┌─────────────────────┐
│                     │
│   HAPPYLAND         │
│                     │
│   Admit One         │
│                     │
│                     │
│     Opens at        │
│     midnight        │
│                     │
└─────────────────────┘
```

CHAPTER 2

Tickets. Jet black like the envelope, the words the same sticky blood red as the handwriting on the front.

"This must be a joke," I muttered. I looked over my shoulder and around the pier. But there was no one else in sight. Not a single friend, or enemy.

The place was dead.

"Maybe," Emma said. "But it's sooooo cool!" She snatched a ticket and stretched it out in front of her face. "A midnight visit to Happyland? That's a seriously awesome birthday present. And who was that clown? He was pretty freaky, right?"

"Hmmmm," Lucas said. "I don't think I want to know. Maybe those tickets are actually meant for someone else."

"Someone called Toby?" Emma said, eyebrow raised.

"There's got to be more than one Toby in Weirville ..." Lucas countered.

"With a birthday today?" Emma said.

"Could be," Lucas said.

"An *eleventh* birthday?" Emma pointed at the card with the big 11 on it, then crossed her arms and tapped her foot.

"Well, uh ..." Lucas tailed off.

Emma was right. If it was a coincidence, it was a pretty huge one.

I glanced at my watch just as the minute hand

twitched to twelve. Suddenly I remembered – we were going to be late.

"Come on," I said. "Mum wanted us home at four."

"Where do you losers think you're going?" Keira yelled as we started to walk back. She blocked our way, planting her hands on her hips.

"Home," I told her.

"Not yet you're not." She thrust out her hand. "First I want my ticket."

"*Your* ticket?" I said.

"Yeah, *genius*, my ticket. There are four tickets and four of us. One each." She scowled at me.

I scowled back. "Are you going to leave us alone if I give you one?"

"Like I want to hang around with you."

I peeled a ticket from my hand and shoved it into hers. "Fine," I said. "Bye, Keira."

"Yeah, see you at midnight. Unless you're too scared." She raised her arms and staggered around like a zombie, tongue lolling, then stuffed the ticket in her pocket and ran away cackling.

"What a cow," Lucas muttered, once she was well out of earshot.

I nodded. "Come on," I said. "Mum's made cake."

As we walked down the pier, I took one look back at the deserted Happyland. It hung over us like a dark cloud in an otherwise sunny sky. Nothing moved except a torn candyfloss banner that flapped helplessly against an empty snack stand. Of all the places for my ball to land. The fiery pits of hell would've been more welcoming.

"You're late," Mum said. She slashed at my birthday cake with a long, sharp knife. "Where were you?"

"We were just down by the old pier, playing foot—" Emma began.

I kicked Emma under the table and shook my head.

"... ball."

"The pier?" Mum's voice raised a notch. "I told you never to go near that place." She stabbed a piece of cake and slapped it on a plate. Bits of icing flew from the blade. She sliced out another hunk. And another. Until all that was left of my birthday cake was a jagged square.

"We weren't on the pier, Mum," I said. "Just playing on the beach. We stayed there the whole time. Really."

"Yeah, Mrs M., we were just on the beach," Emma chimed in.

Mum set down the knife and stared at the mangled cake. She sucked in a deep breath, wiped away a tear and left the dining room without a word. I heard water run and dishes clatter in the kitchen, followed by sniffles.

"I've never seen your mum get angry about you being a few minutes late," said Lucas. "It's only ten past."

"Well, they don't call this town Weirdsville for nothing," I said, trying to make light of things. I'd given up trying to work out adults. I was about to eat the sugar-paper number eleven when I remembered: Mum's sister, Camille, disappeared on her eleventh birthday, when Mum was just ten.

My heart sank and I started to feel really guilty for making Mum worry. And even more for dredging up memories. Bad ones.

We finished the cake and headed upstairs to my room. Lucas and Emma were staying the night, so we had hours to do whatever we wanted.

But all we could think about was that envelope of tickets.

"How long has that place been closed?" Emma asked. She sat on my beanbag chair, bouncing a football on her knees. My *old* ball. The lame one.

"Basically for ever," Lucas said. He dropped a handful of food pellets into my fish tank and shook the container for more.

Emma kicked the ball away and pulled out her camera phone. "I think we should go. Imagine the footage I could get. It'll be epic!"

"But Toby's mum said we should never go near, and mine always says that too," Lucas said, jiggling the fish food container.

"When did that ever stop us?" Emma countered. "Are you scared?"

"Course not." Lucas kept his back turned and

dumped another pile of food into the tank. The fish went wild. I grabbed the container from him and plonked it on my chest of drawers before he fed them all to death.

Emma jumped off the beanbag and did a little dance in front of Lucas. "Ooooh," she whined. "Happy the Clown's gonna get me. Didn't you see him at the pier, waving? I'm sooooo scared."

"Shut up." Lucas elbowed Emma and she stumbled sideways. "I'm not scared!"

"Yes you are!"

"No I'm not!"

"Are so."

They shot insults back and forth for the next five minutes. It felt like an hour. I started playing on my Nintendo until they went quiet. When I looked up from my game they were staring at me.

"What?" I said.

"It's up to you then, Toby," Lucas said.

Emma grinned and nodded, waving her camera phone in the air. Lucas pinched his lips tight and tried not to pull his terrified look: the face he always makes when Keira's around. I took the ticket from my pocket and wondered why that clown had sent the balloon. There had to be a reason. Then, there was my ball. My brand new perfect ball . . .

Emma tapped her foot.

. . . a hand-stitched Nike T90 . . .

"OK," I said. "But not until my parents are asleep."

"Yessssss!" said Emma and held up her hand for a high five.

I slapped her palm, then noticed Lucas, who'd gone even paler than usual. I felt bad again – but hopefully a trip to Happyland would be good for

him. Dad's always saying it's important to face your fears.

I took one more look at my ticket, turning it over and over in my hand until the writing was smudged and the tips of my fingers were stained.

Blood red.

Emma was gone. Again. I was starting to feel like this trip wasn't such a great idea. What if my parents woke up and realised we weren't in bed? I banished that thought and peered through the gloom up and down the deserted beach. But it was hard to make out what was what in the dark, and now we were almost at the pier. It was eerily still in this part of town, with no sounds but the crashing waves. As if nothing dared move. Not a good time for Emma to wander off with her camera phone. I shivered, sucked in a deep breath and whistled.

There was a crunching of sand behind us, and Lucas and I whirled round to see Emma run up, breathless.

"You wouldn't believe the shots I just got of this fox," she puffed. "Snuck right up on it."

"A fox?" I said. "Unbelievable. What was it before, a crooked tree? A pile of bin bags?"

Emma thumped my arm.

"Just see if I thank you in my Oscar speech." She grinned.

Lucas's mouth stayed drawn in a tight line.

"C'mon, Lucas," I said. "It's my birthday. Cheer up!"

Lucas shook his head. "I can hear something," he said in a low whisper.

"It's probably just Emma's fox," I said. "Wants that video destroyed before he ends up on YouTube."

Emma giggled.

"No, Toby," he said. "I hear something. *Listen.*"

We stopped. The beach was quiet. Until a shrill voice broke the silence.

"*Woooooo!*" it howled. "*Woooooo!* Toooooobeeeeeeee!"

I froze. Emma and Lucas grabbed my arms. I stood tall and puffed out my chest, even though my heart was thumping so hard I thought it might eject itself right out of my ribcage.

"Who is it?" I said in the toughest voice I could come up with.

No answer.

"Is someone there?"

Not a sound. Not even a seagull's screech.

Suddenly, something lunged at us from the darkness.

Emma, Lucas and I jumped. Lucas's fingers dug into my arm. Emma choked back a scream. Then she scowled.

Keira stood in front of us, dressed in a black hoodie, doubled over laughing.

"I didn't think you chickens would actually have the guts to show up here tonight," she said. "If you weren't such losers, I'd be impressed."

Emma's scowl deepened and Lucas tightened his grip on my arm. I shook him loose.

"Good one, Keira." There was no way she was going to see how scared I'd been. I crossed my arms over my chest, but Keira kept howling.

"OK, great to see you," I said. "Safe journey home, now."

"Home?" She waved her black ticket in the air. "No way. I'm going to ride on that roller coaster. Or die trying." She sniggered.

I shrugged. "Do what you like."

We walked along, hoping that Keira would give up

and go home. But instead, she followed us, making spooky noises and chuckling to herself.

Finally the pier emerged out of the darkness, looming like Castle Dracula. The sea was choppy for this time of year and the waves crashed against the posts.

None of us said a word. I took a deep breath and headed for the pier entrance. Nothing had changed from earlier. The fence stood as it had before with the sign warning us to stay away. We took a few steps on the boards, the wood planks creaking beneath our feet. The rotting pier dipped and sagged. Every step felt one step closer to plunging into the waves and getting sucked out to sea.

"What now?" Emma asked when we reached the fence. She peered up at the huge tangle of mesh and barbed wire.

"Might as well go back," Lucas said. "No way over that thing." He shrugged and started walking away.

I grabbed him by the sleeve.

"There's always a way," I said, pointing to a gap in the barbed wire.

I stuck my foot in a chain link and hoisted myself up and over, through the gap. Emma followed. Then Keira. Lucas hesitated, glanced anxiously around the empty pier, then scurried over and began to climb.

The park looked even darker and spookier in the dead of night. Moonlight cast weird shadows off the empty booths and deserted rides. The only sound came from the violent waves and wind whistling down the pathways.

We approached the turnstiles. I pulled the black

tickets from my pocket and hesitated. Lucas breathed heavily beside me. Even Keira's face was pinched.

"Right," I said. "We've come this far." I jammed a ticket into the turnstile. "It probably won't work any—"

The machine sucked up my ticket then showed a display saying Enter. Something inside it clicked, as if unlocking.

"Whoa!" gasped Emma.

One by one the lights on the stalls flickered, then turned on. Music started slowly, like an old-fashioned gramophone, speeding up into a wacky carnival tune. Rides started moving. Lights flashed.

Emma staggered backward, muttering to herself. An eerie glow lit her shocked face. Lucas just stood there, dumbfounded, a swirl of colours reflecting off his thick glasses. Even Keira was speechless.

"OK," I said, swallowing hard. "The lights are on ..."

Someone must be home.

CHAPTER 3

Happyland was open for business. For the first time since ... well ... who knew?

"Who do you think's running this place?" I asked the others.

They stared blankly back at me.

"I'm in if you're in," said Keira, but her voice shook a little.

"Fine then," I said. "I'm in. As long as we stick together, we'll be OK." I held out my right hand. "Deal?"

"Deal," Keira said. She put her hand on top of mine.

"Deal." Emma placed her hand in the circle.

Lucas stared at us, chewing his lip. Finally, he put his shaking hand on top of Emma's, then immediately snatched it back.

We lined up at the turnstiles. The others put their tickets in. We looked at each other, then pushed the creaking, rotating bars, and entered. We were inside Happyland.

On the other side stood a three-metre statue of Happy the Clown, faded with age, gashes of paint missing from its dull white cheeks. Birds – or something else, I didn't really want to know what – had picked away most of the orange hair, leaving just a few scraggly tufts coming out of the statue's head. A faded blue eye stared at us. Its only eye.

With a jolt, the red-painted mouth flopped open.

"Welcome to Happyland!" a tinny voice said. "Where the fun never ends . . ."

The statue's mechanical arm jerked up and down while its eye twitched left and right, then rolled back in its rusted socket.

"Forget it. I'm off," Lucas said in a terrified squeak. Next thing I knew, he was running for the turnstiles.

"Hey!" I grabbed him by his backpack. Lucas carried that thing *everywhere*. "What did I say about sticking together?"

"I'm sorry, Toby," Lucas mumbled. "But this place is too weird. I'm going home!" He shook his head, eyes still wide, his lips trembling.

Just then, there was a click and a flash. Lucas blinked. I turned to see Keira holding Emma's phone high above her head. Emma leapt and grabbed for it, but missed and came back down with nothing.

"Great picture, Lucas Pukas," Keira said. She spun the phone so we could all see Lucas's terrified face filling the screen. "Unless you'd like your snivelling scaredy-cat mug posted online tomorrow for the whole school to see, I suggest you come with us." She smirked.

Lucas's shoulders slumped. "Fine," he sighed.

Keira tossed Emma her phone. We shuffled past the now-silent Happy the Clown statue and an ancient board covered with peeling pictures of smiling children. "Get a photo with every ride!" faded letters exclaimed below.

"Look, Pukas!" Keira pointed at the sign. "Say cheese!"

Lucas glared at her but said nothing.

We continued down the main path, lined with brightly coloured stalls and hand-painted signs pointing out the attractions. Carnival music and the whir of spinning rides filled the air, occasionally broken by disembodied shrieks of thrill and terror. Which was strange, because as far as I could tell, we were the only ones here.

"What should we do first?" I said.

"Let's go on a ride!" Emma said.

"I bet that roller coaster goes properly fast," Keira said.

I realised I could smell popcorn. Fresh, buttered popcorn. My stomach grumbled.

"Let's get a snack first," I suggested.

I headed over to a nearby stall. Popcorn bags of all different flavours lined the shelves – buttered, salt, toffee ... I licked my lips. What to choose?

Suddenly, a boy rose up from behind the counter. I leaned back on my heels.

"Whoa! Didn't see you there, mate," I said.

"Welcome to Happyland," the boy replied, in a flat voice. He looked anything but happy. Pale, with dark shadows under his eyes, the poor kid seemed exhausted. He wore a bright red-and-blue-striped uniform that was about six sizes too big. His slick brown hair was parted down the middle and combed flat. Weird. Only time I'd ever seen a boy with a hairstyle like that was in pictures of my dad and his friends when he was younger.

"Uh, thanks," I said. "One buttered popcorn please."

The boy turned away and grabbed a bag, his thin arm poking like a toothpick from his oversized sleeve.

"So how long have you been working here?" I asked.

"Twenty years," he said.

He pushed the popcorn towards me, unsmiling.

"Good one," I chuckled. It was a weird joke, but I didn't want to be rude. "Bet it feels like that, right?"

The boy just stared at me blankly. Oh well, life must be pretty lame if you're working the night shift and can't have any fun. I cleared my throat.

"So how much is that?"

"Nothing," he said.

"Really? It's free?"

"Don't worry," the boy answered in his monotone voice. "You'll pay later."

Goosebumps sprang up on my arms. I muttered thanks and dodged off to join my friends. Keira and Lucas were standing in front of a huge park map. Lucas was running his finger along the board, silently mouthing the names of rides.

"Hey, swot," Keira snorted. "This isn't Boy Scouts."

"I just think it would be good to know where we're

going," Lucas said, still tracing his way over the map. We huddled in closer to look, following Lucas's shaky finger. HAPPY'S GHOST TRAIN. HAPPY'S CRAZY MAZE. At the end of the pier, Lucas's finger came to a stop on a faded drawing of the big top – HAPPY'S FUNHOUSE. Lucas yelped and yanked his hand back, shaking it as though something had just bitten him.

"What's the matter?" I asked, stuffing a handful of popcorn in my mouth. This place couldn't be all bad. The food was good, at least. I held out the bag and gave it a little shake. "Want some?"

Lucas shook his head and flipped his hand over. A jagged sliver of wood stuck from his fingertip. His face had turned white.

"It's just a splinter," I said. "You'll live." I grabbed his hand and yanked the shard out. A small crimson bubble formed in its place. Lucas popped his finger in his mouth and blinked at me from behind his black-rimmed glasses.

"OK, what nex—"

"Ow!" Emma shouted. She was standing over by a coconut booth, rubbing her head. "Keira, I know you don't like me, but do you really have to throw things at me?"

"What are you talking about, weirdo?" Keira said. "I've been watching Pukas cry over a splinter."

Lucas frowned.

"Give it a rest, Keira," I said. "What happened, Em?"

"I don't know," she said. "I threw a ball at a coconut. And then something hit *me* in the back of the head." She glared at Keira.

Keira snorted. "That's funny. Wish I *had* thought of it."

I grabbed one of the faded blue balls and chucked

it at a coconut. *Pow!* Something whacked me on the back of the head and I stumbled forward.

"Ouch!" I said. "What the . . . ?"

"See!" Emma said.

"Yeah, I see," Keira said. "It's official. You two are completely mental." She scooped up a ball and hurled it at the booth. Almost immediately her hand flew to her head. "Hey," she shouted, glancing around. "Who did that?"

Lucas glared at all of us. I could tell he was dying to say I told you so.

Apart from the four of us, there was no one in sight. Even that freaky kid from the popcorn stand had disappeared. An empty plastic bag skittered across the path. I smelled something. But it wasn't the sweet smell of fairground food any more. It was something gross, decaying and rotten. Like dead fish. Or worse.

Suddenly my popcorn seemed about as appetising as a bag of worms, and I chucked it in the nearest bin.

OK, maybe there *was* something strange about this place.

Maybe our parents had a good reason for telling us to stay away.

A cold breeze blew across the amusement park and in the distance, something metal clicked and locked.

It sounded like the turnstiles.

Shutting us in.

CHAPTER 4

"Can we all agree this was a bad idea now?" said Lucas, sucking on his bloodied finger. "Why don't we just go? Before something *really* bad happens?"

"I guess—" I started to say. But I was interrupted by a girl's voice.

"Go where?" she said.

We spun around to see a kid our age standing in the middle of the path, an oversized Happyland uniform hanging from her thin shoulders. A clown nametag pinned to her chest read MILLY. She was pale, just like that boy at the popcorn stand, and she looked vaguely familiar. Maybe the popcorn boy's twin sister. She did have the same black circles beneath her eyes, the same blank expression and the same monotone voice. Her dark hair hung in two neatly braided pigtails, really reminding me of someone . . .

"We were just getting ready to leave," Lucas said.

"*Leave?*" Milly said. "Why? This place is fun."

"Fun," Lucas grumbled under his breath. "You lot have a weird idea of fun around here."

"What, are you chicken or something?" Milly challenged. "You should at least try one ride before you go." She stared at us, unblinking.

"Ooh, yeah . . . one ride!" Keira and Emma said in unison, then looked at each other with surprise. I'm not sure what was more shocking – the fact that they

wanted to stay – or that they actually agreed on something for once. Whatever. I wasn't going to be the one to wimp out. I knew that much.

"One ride sounds good," I said. "Besides, we still need to find my ball. Right, Lucas?"

Lucas glared at me.

"Lucas?" I elbowed him.

"OK," he said. "As long as we stick together, right?"

"Right," I said.

"Oh, whatever, Pukas," Keira said with a roll of her eyes. "So, where to?"

"May I suggest Happy's Ghost Train?" Milly said. "That would be an excellent place to start." She pointed towards the old wooden roller coaster in the distance. The rickety tracks rose high into the sky, jutting out over the churning sea. They seemed to sway with every gust of wind. I shivered. The ride looked about as stable as a house built from tooth-picks.

Emma glanced up and bit her lip. "I don't know," she said. "You sure that thing's safe?"

"Of course," Milly said. "No one's ever left Happyland ... injured." She motioned us forward with a wave of her pale hand. "This way."

Milly led us through the main avenue to the other side of the park. As we walked, I couldn't help but feel sorry for the girl, the way her shoulders slumped and her feet dragged across the ground. Maybe she was a little freaky, but she still looked, well, kind of sad.

We reached the Ghost Train entrance, which had been set up to look like an actual train station. Of course, not any old station. According to the sign, we had just arrived at TERROR JUNCTION to take train number 666, departing at the stroke of midnight. A

Happy the Clown robot, clad in a striped conductor's hat, sat behind a ticket booth. Its mouth flopped open and the head creaked back and forth.

"Last call for the Ghost Train!" it said. "Boarding on track number thirteen! Enter if you dare!"

Lucas recoiled. "I. Don't. Like. This."

"Why don't you go join your friends, then?" Keira said. She pointed at a group of skeletons in business suits perched on a nearby bench.

"No thanks." Lucas reached into his backpack and produced a faded baseball cap. He'd been wearing it the only time he'd ever won anything – a guess-how-many-balls-in-the-jar contest back when we were six. Now it was his lucky hat. Though what it had done for him since, I'm not sure. Mostly just wrecked his chances of ever getting a girl to like him. He plopped it on his head and kept walking, shoulders hunched.

43

"The hat's not gonna help you, Pukas," crowed Keira. "Last I heard, ghosts aren't scared of lame."

We ignored her and followed Milly through the empty rope line, back and forth until we reached the boarding area. A makeshift train car sat on the track ahead, HAPPY'S GHOST TRAIN scrawled across the side. Well, at least that's what I thought it said. It was kind of hard to tell. Most of the letters looked like they'd been clawed away, and there were scratch marks in the paint. Hopefully not left by the last person to ride the thing.

"All aboard," Milly said. She unlatched the rope and gestured us forward. Keira shoved her way in first and plopped into the front of the empty carriage.

"Shotgun!" she said, pumping her fist in the air. "Yes!"

Lucas followed, climbing in the middle, muttering

something about velocity, centrifugal forces and stability. I sat next to him. Emma slid in beside me. She was trying to peer around the side of the entrance at the swooping wooden roller coaster drop over the sea.

"That looks pretty high, right?" she said.

"I guess," I said. "It *is* a roller coaster."

"Yeah," she answered, looking strangely pale. She held the phone up and pushed record. But before she could say anything, Keira's big mug popped up in front.

"Hey there, everybody! This is Emma, Toby, Lucas and ... Keira! About to embark on the ride of a lifetime ... Happy's Ghost Train!" The metal safety bar creaked into place, pinning us to our seats. I looked back at the platform to see Milly still standing there, rope dangling from her hand.

"Hey," I said. "Aren't you going to get on?"

45

She shook her head. "No thanks. I've done this a thousand times before."

"You can't have actually ridden it *a thousand* times," said Lucas.

"One thousand, four hundred and eighty-three times," she said.

"What?" I began to say, but before I could finish, Milly pulled a lever and the carriage jerked forward. Our heads jolted.

"Whoa!" Emma said with a nervous giggle.

"Woo-hoo!" Keira yelled, throwing her hands above her head.

The carriage creaked up a tall slope of track, then turned into a dark tunnel. It took a minute for my eyes to adjust. When they did, I could see the black walls were painted with leafless trees. Luminescent eyeballs glowed in the branches. But the paint was so old and chipped, the whole thing looked more like a faded mural in a nursery. Well, maybe the nursery of some demon baby. Still, it wasn't exactly scary.

The carriage bumped and rattled. Something metal broke loose and clanked noisily through the open track below.

Lucas jumped. "What was that?"

I didn't have time to wonder as the carriage jerked once more and the ride sped up. The tunnel darkened. The sound of wind blowing and thunder cracking filled the narrow space, but it was obviously just sound effects. Emma sighed and glanced at her camera phone. She was looking a little more relaxed now that the ride had begun.

"This isn't scary enough," she said. "My film is going to be so rub—" She jumped back in her seat, stopped by a sudden beating of wings. A swarm of

screeching black bats filled the tunnel, swooping directly above us. I could've sworn a sharp claw scraped the top of my head. I ran my fingers through my hair. It couldn't be ... I mean, what sort of ghost train had *real bats*? I looked at Lucas. His eyes were squeezed shut and he was muttering something to himself again. Probably praying to his lucky hat.

"What's wrong, Pukas?" Keira said. "Bat got your tongue?"

Lucas opened one eye and glared at her.

Somewhere above our heads, a tinny speaker crackled and popped into life.

Happy the Clown's voice blared over it. "Welcome to the Haunted House!" he said. "Come on in and stay a while ... Hahahahahahahahahaha ...!" With that, a skeleton dangling from a noose swung from the ceiling and waved back and forth in front of our carriage.

A set of thick wooden doors straight ahead groaned open. We jerked inside.

The carriage slowed. We were in the entrance of a creepy old Victorian-style house. Dusty oriental rugs lined the floor. Suits of armour wielding swords and axes in gauntleted hands stood at attention along the walls. High above our heads, a rusted old chandelier held dozens of burning yellowed candles. I watched the light flicker and wondered how those things got lit. And who lit them . . .

The carriage turned and rolled past a line of knights holding their weapons high in the air, ready to strike.

"Man," Lucas said, eyeballing a glinting axe blade. "Those things look totally real."

"Oh, sure, wimp," Keira said sarcastically. "They're real all right. So real I can do this." She stuck out her

hand and grabbed the blade. "Ouch!" she yelped, quickly yanking her hand back.

She stared at the thin line of blood that ran from her finger, down her palm and on to her wrist. A tiny crimson dot landed on the carriage seat. Lucas crossed his arms and thrust his chin forward.

"Told you," he said. Keira grimaced and rubbed her hand.

"I don't get it," I said. "Why would a ride like this have real axes on it? It doesn't make any sense ... "

As if in some sort of twisted answer, the blade swung down fast. Lucas ducked, his hat flew off his head, and the blade sliced off the visor in mid-air.

"Whoa!" I said, heart pounding. "What was that?"

"The axe! It just fell!" said Lucas.

"You must have nudged it," said Emma.

"I didn't!" he said. "I swear!" He looked back at the

remains of his lucky cap. *"Let's just take one ride!"* he muttered to himself, picking up the two bits. "One ride . . . sure. OK! That'll be loads of fun!"

Our carriage lurched forward again. Emma and Lucas exchanged worried looks. I tried not to act too concerned, but clearly that axe was real.

Did that mean the others were too?

I just knew one thing – I wasn't about to stay on the train and find out.

CHAPTER 5

I reached over Emma to the side of the carriage and unlatched the safety bar.

"Hey," Emma said. "Keep your hands and feet inside the car at all times!"

"Ha ha," I said, pushing the bar open. "This thing isn't safe. We need to get off."

I climbed out. The rest of them just sat there as the carriage cranked slowly forward. "Well?" I said. "You coming?"

Lucas scrambled over Emma's lap, kicking Keira in the process. "Don't have to ask me twice," he said. Emma shrugged and followed him.

Keira swatted at Lucas's flailing leg. "Oh, all right." She stood and promptly tripped as she climbed out. "Ooof!" she said as her combat boots slammed on to the floor. Dust puffed from the carpet.

The carriage disappeared into the darkness.

We raced back towards the doors the carriage had come through, dodging past the suits of armour and along the carpeted hallway. But just as we reached them, the doors banged shut, sucking the air from the room with a whoosh. The candles flickered out. We were plunged into complete darkness.

"You've got to be kidding me," Emma groaned. She flipped open her phone and pointed the dim light straight ahead.

Lucas hurled himself at the doors, shaking the handles as hard as his bony arms would allow, shrieking, "Let me out of here!" The doors didn't budge. Emma, Keira and I joined him, pulling the handles as hard as we could. Useless.

At last we gave up and turned back to face the haunted house, lit only by Emma's phone and sounding eerily silent without the clanking carriage wheels. The air was musty and damp.

"This place is disgusting," I said, pinching my nose. "It smells like an old shoe."

"Or the inside of a coffin," Keira snorted.

Lucas let out a small whimper.

"Well, if we can't go back," I said, "we're just going to have to go forward."

"Oh, yay," Lucas said.

We followed the narrow square of light from

Emma's phone along the empty tracks, through the hallway and into a narrow corridor. Old-fashioned portraits lined the walls. It was probably safe to say the eyes were following us, but I didn't look to find out. This place was creepy enough as it was. We passed more suits of armour, each one sporting weaponry. Axes. Swords. Pikes. Shields. Lucas kept his arms tight to his side, still grumbling under his breath. It didn't help that Keira was pausing every ten seconds to admire the gear.

"Check out this one!" she said, stopping before a massive suit of polished armour. She slowly extended her hand to it. "This is so cool. I'm going to try it on."

I grabbed her arm. "Forget it," I said. "We should get out of here."

"Oh, c'mon," Keira said. "You're such a load of boring wusses!"

"And you're crazy," Lucas said. "Didn't you learn anything the last time you touched one of those things?"

"Don't be such a wimp, Pukas," Keira said. She unhooked a belted scabbard and fastened it around her waist. The sword made an icy hiss as she drew it.

"Ha!" she said, slicing the air in front of her. Emma, Lucas and I jumped back a step. A piece of the track cracked beneath our feet.

"I don't feel safe in here," Emma said, gripping my arm.

"Fear not!" Keira said, like she was from the Middle Ages or something. "I will protect you with my trusty sword!" She brandished the blade above her head, nearly catching Lucas by the ear. He dodged sideways just in time. I guess all those years of ducking every time a ball flew his way had finally paid off.

"Yeah," Emma said. "It's because of you and your *trusty sword* I don't feel safe!"

Keira huffed and forged ahead, swishing the sword in front of her. "In the name of the Queen, I take this land ... "

Suddenly, she let out an ear-piercing shrick.

Emma, Lucas and I jolted to a stop. Usually wails of fear are aimed at Keira – they don't come from her. Emma shone her phone light up ahead. Keira was spinning around on tiptoe, arms flailing, eyes squeezed shut. A black carpet of shapes had unrolled across the floor and writhed around her feet. My eyes adjusted and finally I could see what had Keira so freaked out.

Rats. Hundreds and hundreds of mangy, squirming rats.

"Get them off me!" yelled Keira. "Get them off me!"

But the rats continued to surge across the path in one massive chattering wave of matted fur and stringy tails. They freaked me out and I stood on one leg, trying not to touch them. But the way Keira danced about like her boots were on fire was quite funny. I'd never seen such fast footwork from her, even on the football field.

"Ewwww ... ewwww ... ewwww!" she squealed as the rats spilled across her feet.

Finally, the last one scuttled past and disappeared into a dark corner. The chattering stopped. Keira slowly opened one eye.

"Are they gone?" she said, still quivering and kicking at the empty space around her.

"Yeah, they're gone," Emma said. "But this isn't." She held out her phone so we could all see the recording of Keira, squealing and shaking in her combat boots. Her hands swung wildly, swatting imaginary rodents from her black clothes.

Emma and I laughed at her. But I did also have a quick look round to make sure they were *definitely* all gone.

"Gimme that thing!" Keira said, swiping the air with a still-trembling hand.

"Forget it." Emma stuffed the phone in her pocket. "This is too good!"

Keira scowled. Emma smirked. I was surprised Lucas wasn't howling with laughter. The guy had waited all of Year 6 – no wait – his entire life to see Keira Ramone knocked down a peg.

"Hey, Lucas," I said, chuckling. But he didn't answer.

"Lucas?" I squinted into the darkness. He was nowhere in sight. That was weird. Mr As-Long-As-

We-All-Stick-Together was the last person I expected to wander off. Especially in here.

"Lucas!" I yelled. Emma joined in. But there was nothing but a mocking echo in response.

Lucas, Lucas, Lucas . . .

"C'mon, Lucas," Emma said, searching behind the rows of armour. "If you're hiding, this isn't funny!"

A knot formed in my stomach. I knew the last thing Lucas would do was hide, especially not in a haunted house. He usually refused to play hide and seek back when we were little. OK, so maybe once I accidentally left him "hiding" under our dark porch when Mum called me in for tea. But, still, it's not exactly my fault he stayed there for three hours.

"Lucas?" I called out again.

This time, it was Emma who answered with a terrified shout.

"Over here!" she yelled.

Keira and I ran to where Emma stood in the shadows. She pointed to a small skeleton in school uniform slumped against the wall. It was propped between two suits of armour, head bent unnaturally on its exposed ribcage. A plump black spider crawled through the skeleton's eye socket and up a massive web that ran the full length of the wall. I shuddered.

"Lucas?" Emma said, shaking.

"C'mon, Em, that can't be Lucas," I said. "That thing's obviously been there for years. Besides, Lucas wasn't wearing a uniform. None of us are."

"But he was wearing *this*," she said. She held out part of Lucas's baseball cap.

The skeleton wobbled and fell over in a cloud of dust.

I swallowed, and crouched down beside the pile of

bones. They were shiny. "Look," I said. "It's not even real. It's just plastic. A toy!"

"Really?" said Emma, obviously relieved.

"Easy mistake to make, though," Keira said. "The resemblance to your bony little mate is uncanny."

"Not funny," Emma said. She turned her back on Keira. "But where *is* he?"

"I think it's a pretty safe bet he didn't run ahead of us," I said. "We'll have to go back."

"Fantastic," Keira grumbled.

We'd made it all of three steps when something creaked up ahead. Keira stood on tiptoe, shuffling and scanning the ground for the first sign of a rodent attack.

Emma shook her head. "I don't think it's a rat." She pointed. "Not unless it's a really big one!"

A shadowy figure wearing a suit of armour stepped

out of the darkness and clanked to a stop, blocking our path. The thing stood almost two metres tall and held a shield on one arm and clutched a massive sword in his other. A dented helmet, jutting to a point, completely covered its head.

Keira leaned back on her heels and laughed. "Good one, Lucas!" she said. "Maybe you're not such a wimp after all."

Lucas's head creaked slowly left and right, but he didn't step forward. Maybe he couldn't move. After all, Lucas was a lot shorter than that suit.

Keira's eyes lit up. She hoisted her sword in the air. "Let's duel!" she said.

Without a word, Lucas lifted his sword in response.

"Wait!" I said. I had a very bad feeling about this. Lucas could barely raise a cricket bat, let alone a broadsword. "I don't think that's such a good—"

But it was too late. Keira had already charged forward, sword swinging, boots stomping.

"You're finished, nerd!" she yelled.

With barely a flinch, Lucas sidestepped Keira's sword and swung his own. Metal clanked as he pushed her blade towards the floor. Keira stumbled backward, flustered.

"Whoa," Emma said. "When did Lucas take up fencing?"

"He didn't." I shook my head. Something was wrong. Very, very wrong.

CHAPTER 6

"All right, wimp," Keira said. "Think you're all tough in the metal suit, huh? Take this!"

She raised her sword and rushed at him. Again, Lucas deflected Keira's attack and bonked her on the head with his gauntlet. I shot Emma a worried look. Lucas may have spent all of his school life dreaming about knocking Keira one on the noggin, but I don't think he'd ever actually do it.

Keira rubbed her head again and glared at him.

"Now you've really done it, Pukas," she said. She took a step back, growled and barrelled straight at him.

Lucas set his feet wide, hoisted his sword and with one slice knocked Keira's weapon from her hand. Then he thrust the sword just over her head, pinning her to the wall by her hoodie. Keira glanced sideways at the glinting blade protruding just centimetres from her ear. Her face went pale. A single drop of sweat rolled down her cheek.

"Whoa," she stammered. "Best of three?"

Lucas pressed forward and clamped his gauntlet around her throat.

"OK, then. You win, mate," Keira gulped.

Lucas didn't budge.

"Lucas, please!" Keira said, eyes bulging. If anything she looked even more scared than she had been with the rats. But still, Lucas didn't let up.

"Hey, Lucas, c'mon," I said. "It's not funny any more."

"Yeah, seriously, Lucas," Emma said. "Let her go."

"Let who go?" a voice said from somewhere in the darkness. A thin figure carrying a backpack emerged from the gloom.

Lucas.

"Sorry, guys," he said, pushing his glasses up the bridge of his nose. "Have you seen the other part of my cap? Got a little lost back there. Did you know they have an actual first-century Roman legionnaire's belt here? Unbelievable! That thing's got to be worth a fortune!" He stopped, noticing Keira, still pinned to the wall. "Hey, what's going on?"

I wasn't entirely sure I wanted to know the answer.

The armoured figure let go of Keira's throat, leaving her panting for breath. There was silence as his head creaked left and right. Then, mad laughter came from beneath his helmet. Growing louder. And louder.

Slowly, the visor creaked open. The robotic face of Happy the Clown peered out. Its eyes glowed red.

"Surprise!" it said, still cackling.

Yeah, that was kind of an understatement.

The robot pointed at Lucas. "See, you thought I was your friend, not some robot. Funny, wasn't it?" We all stayed frozen, afraid to move a millimetre. We definitely didn't laugh. The robot looked back and forth. "What? Kids these days don't enjoy a good joke," it said, red eyes flashing. The voice squeaked higher with every word, like that suit was outfitted with its own helium tank or something. "Oh well, let's see how funny you find this then."

With that, the robot let out a high-pitched whistle. Emma's hands flew over her ears, and I winced and

turned away. That whistle was almost as loud as mine.

The sound intensified until it was replaced by a scurrying whoosh.

Rats.

Surging at us from all sides. I leapt backward.

Keira screamed. She wriggled her arms out of her hoodie, leaving it pinned to the wall as she slipped to the floor and grabbed her sword. Eyes closed, Keira slashed the blade at the screeching, chattering rodents. "Ewwww, ewwww, ewwwwwww!" she yelled. It was useless. More and more rats flooded the room like water bursting through a dam. They were even scrambling on top of each other. In minutes, they'd be stacked to the ceiling.

There was no time to waste.

"Run!" I yelled.

I grabbed Lucas. Emma pulled Keira away from the

wall. The four of us pelted our way further into the depths of the haunted house until Happy's robotic laughter had faded away behind us. The only sound now was our feet slapping against the creaky floorboards, plus the occasional wheeze from Lucas. The darkness intensified the deeper we ran. The air grew colder. There was no end in sight. It was like we were being swallowed whole.

A rat scuttled past and Keira slowed, choking back a scream.

"C'mon, keep moving!" I pulled her forward.

We ran down a black corridor and emerged in a ghoul's dining room. Fake severed heads sat on dusty plates. At least I hoped they were fake. Lucas bumped the table and a head banged to the floor, rolling slowly to a stop upside down against a chair. He stared in horror. The dead eyes stared back.

"I hate this place!" Lucas wailed. "We're never going to get out of here!"

"Yes, we are!" I grabbed Lucas's arm and pointed. A FIRE EXIT sign marked a door straight ahead.

"We're saved!" Lucas yelled. Without hesitation, he charged at the door and flung it open.

A wave of heat burst through the room.

Lucas screamed as he skidded uncontrollably towards the flames. I leapt forward and grabbed him by the backpack, just before he could fall into the fiery inferno on the other side. Keira slammed the door shut.

Lucas collapsed on the ground, shaking, and Emma knelt by his side.

"You're OK, mate," she said, rubbing his shoulder. But when she looked at me, I could tell she thought he was anything but.

"What was that?" Lucas squeaked.

As if in reply, a maniacal laugh came from behind us. We spun around to see Happy the Clown standing over us, cackling. How did he catch up so quickly? But as I got a better look, I saw this wasn't the robot.

It was the real Happy the Clown.

The one from the pier this afternoon.

The one I was pretty sure had sent that black envelope in the first place.

Only up close, he didn't exactly look happy. His orange hair shot wildly in every direction. His white clown makeup was peeling away, revealing chunks of dull grey skin underneath. And his eyes. His eyes glowed blood red. I had to look away. It was like staring directly into an endless burning pit.

"Hahahahahahaha!" Happy said, grinning. "'Fire exit' – get it? That was a good one, wasn't it?" He

slapped his oversized polka-dot clown trousers. A rat scrambled out from the pocket.

Keira gagged. Lucas whimpered next to me. I summoned my courage and puffed out my chest.

"No, it wasn't!" I said. "It wasn't funny at all."

Happy turned his red-painted mouth downward into an exaggerated frown and rubbed mock tears from the corners of his black-rimmed eyes. I looked back at my best friend, still cowering in fear. Stupid clown. Nothing more than a big bully.

"What do you want from us, anyway?" I said. "You gave us those tickets, right? Why?"

Happy just grinned.

"What is your problem?" I said. "Do you like to torture people or something?"

"Torture?" Happy said. "Why, no! I just want you to have fun!" He burst out into another cackle of crazed laughter. "All the children that come here have fun." His red eyes glowed. "That's why they never leave!"

"You're crazy," Emma said, grabbing my arm. "We *are* leaving. Now."

Happy shook his head slowly, ratty orange hair bobbing, mouth curled into an evil smirk. "I'll tell you when you're leaving," he said.

"Let us out of here!" I yelled, shaking. "Let us out, or … or … "

"Or what?" Happy grinned even wider. "Is that a threat?"

"You can't stop us!" I said.

"I wouldn't be so sure." Happy laughed. The evil sound echoed through the deserted ride.

Lucas put his hands over his head. "I want to go home," he said.

Happy tapped his oversized shoes. "OK, OK," he said. "I can see we've got off on the wrong foot. Didn't you know? We're all about fun here at Happyland! So! I'll make you a deal."

Emma, Lucas, Keira and I looked at each other. I was sure nothing good could come from making a deal with this lunatic.

"There's a photo taken on every ride," Happy continued in his sing-song voice. "Bring me three photos from three different rides. Then, I'll let you go. If you still want to, that is."

Emma leaned over and whispered, "I don't trust this nutter."

"Me neither," I said.

Happy whistled to himself and kept tapping his foot. "Well, I'm waiting," he said. "Will the contestants take door number one? Or two?" He pointed back at the fire exit, put his gloved hand over his mouth and giggled.

Unfortunately, I didn't see what choice we had.

"OK." I frowned at Happy. "We bring you three pictures ... and you let us go, right?"

Happy nodded – a little too happily.

"So what's the catch?" I said.

"Catch?" Happy's black-painted eyebrows shot straight up. "Why, I'm offended. There's no catch!" He grinned broadly, revealing a row of large, yellowed teeth.

I shuddered.

"Fine," I said. "Three rides. Three pictures. Then you let us go."

Happy smiled even wider. "That's the deal!" He clapped his hands.

The roller coaster carriage emerged from the

darkness and cranked slowly up the tracks, stopping directly in front of where we stood. Happy motioned us on board with an oversized glove.

"Off you go now!" he said. "Oh, and maybe if you're lucky, you'll catch this." He reached into his puffy shirt and pulled something out. Something round. And white.

My ball!

Happy lifted his big, red shoe and drop-kicked it into the darkness.

"Hey!" I yelled.

Emma grabbed my arm. "We'll worry about the ball later," she said. "Let's go!"

Keira tucked the sword into her belt, then one by one we stepped back into the carriage. The safety bar slammed shut, pinning us down. The train lurched forward.

"Oh! And did I mention?" Happy called out. "Those pictures? Just one eensy-weensy thing ... Make sure you're smiling. In every one. That means *all* of you!"

The train creaked forward into the blackness.

CHAPTER 7

The wheels clacked louder and louder on the old tracks. The train picked up speed until it was hurtling along at a breakneck pace. Emma pulled out her camera phone and held it high.

"How can you film at a time like this?" I yelled.

"I don't know," Emma shouted back over the clacking of the wheels. The train gained momentum, jerking left and right. "It helps keep my mind off—"

The carriage veered around a corner, nearly tipping

us over the side. My stomach lurched. Keira grunted. Emma jammed her camera phone back in her pocket and clutched the bar.

"Oh forget it!" she screeched as the train shot around another bend. And another. And another. I screwed my eyes shut. We had to be nearing the end of this crazy ride. It couldn't go on for ever, could it?

Suddenly, I felt Keira's thick hand on the back of my neck, followed by a wave of heat above.

"Look out!" she said.

I opened my eyes to see a sheet of flames burst through the air – just as Keira shoved me face first on to the safety bar. In any other situation I might have thought Keira just enjoyed making me eat metal. But not now. As I sat up, sweating, I could see her face was as pale as Lucas's. Suddenly, the train jerked and slowed down.

"Oh, now what?" Lucas said as the train crept forward.

I pointed up ahead, my hand trembling. Further along the track, a guillotine blade sliced through the air, landing on a carriage a few rows ahead and smashing it to bits. If Keira had been riding shotgun, she would have been squashed with it. Keira chewed her bottom lip and stared at the wreckage. Clearly, she was thinking the same thing.

Our carriage jerked forward. The guillotine raised up again, silver blade glinting. Emma, Lucas and Keira lifted the safety bar and scrambled backward in panic.

"No, wait!" I said. "The other way!"

I grabbed Emma's hand and scrambled forward to the carriage ahead. We ducked under the creaking blade.

"Wait, my foot's caught," said Lucas.

I caught hold of his wrist and pulled him forward just as the blade swooped down, annihilating the carriage we'd been sitting in moments earlier.

Lucas turned and looked at me, eyes wide, and didn't say a word. He didn't need to. The tremble of his bottom lip said it all.

The train bumped ahead. We spun around, only to be smacked in the face by something sticky and cold.

Spiderwebs.

The stuff wrapped around us, tangling itself in our hair, eyes and clothes. "That's disgusting," Emma said, spitting. We grabbed handfuls of web and tossed them over the edge. I brushed my shirt and wiped my face, pushing my hands up through my hair.

"Wait! Look out!" Keira yelled.

I froze.

Something was creeping up the back of my neck.

Emma screamed, reached over and flung whatever it was off me. I watched in horror as an eight-legged hairy *thing* hurtled out of the carriage and into the darkness.

"What was that?" I asked, heart pounding.

"Just a little spider, that's all," Emma said with a gulp.

Right. That didn't look like any ordinary house spider. Well, not unless your house was located deep in the underworld. I rubbed my neck. I couldn't shake the feeling that thing was still creeping all over me.

"Thanks, Em," I said with a shudder.

"Well, if your friends won't swat away huge, poisonous spiders, then who will?" Emma said, forcing a laugh.

The train suddenly jolted, and slowed to a crawl. We banged forward in our seats.

"Oh, man," Lucas moaned.

We stopped in front of a set of old wooden doors. A sign hung directly above:

PREPARE FOR THE DEATHLY DROP!

Before we could think about what that meant, the doors swung open and cold sea air blew on our faces. I peered over the edge. Far below, the waves churned and smashed against the rocks. I gulped.

The train lurched out over the sea, up a steep set of rickety tracks, throwing us straight back against our seats. I knew what was coming.

A roller coaster drop.

The train continued its slow creak up the tracks. Usually, this was my favourite part of the ride. But after meeting Happy, I had no idea what to expect. We passed another sign:

SMILE FOR THE CAMERA ON YOUR WAY DOWN!

Wonderful. I checked Lucas to my right. Still pale, but managing a strange sort of lopsided grin. Keira had her hands in the air, waving in anticipation. *Unbelievable.* Then I noticed Emma, trembling beside me. Her temples beaded with sweat and she chewed her bottom lip.

"Whoa," I said. "What's up? Are you OK?"

She shook her head.

"C'mon, Em," I said. "You're not scared of anything!"

"Except heights," she said with a gulp. She was breathing fast, practically panting with fear.

Of course. I couldn't believe I'd forgotten. When Emma was five she spent nearly a whole day lying on the floor of my tree house, afraid to move. Dad finally had to carry her down with a blanket covering her face.

"It's OK, Em," I said, grabbing her hand. "Just close your eyes and try not to think about it."

She shook her head even harder and tightened her white-knuckled grip on the safety bar. "Not. Possible."

"C'mon, Emma," Keira said. "Pull yourself together! If you don't smile, this whole stupid ride will be wasted. You don't want to have to do this again, do you?"

Helpful. Emma just squeaked in response.

The train cranked higher. I couldn't see the end of the tracks any more – there was just black sky, with wispy grey clouds. We had to be almost there.

Something rattled and clanked. I peered over the edge to see a handful of nuts and bolts shake loose and tumble into the darkness. The wooden struts supporting the track creaked and groaned under our carriage.

This was not good.

A loud grind of scraping metal and splintering wood sounded behind us. With a massive screech, a huge section of track broke away. We turned and watched as it crashed into the sea and was swallowed by the waves.

"Uh-oh," Lucas said. "I'm not sure how long this track can maintain sufficient integrity to keep us ... " he gulped. "Up here."

Keira glared at him. "Shut up, nerd."

Emma dropped her head to the safety bar, hyperventilating.

I had to get her to smile. And fast. I didn't like to admit it, but Keira was right – there was no way I wanted to go on this ride again. And now we were nearly at the top.

"Hey, Emma!" I said. "What's the difference between roast beef and pea soup?"

The train continued its deathly grind upward. Emma stayed silent.

"Anyone can roast beef!" I said.

Keira snorted. Even Lucas chuckled. No response from Emma.

"Ooh! I've got one!" Lucas said. "What did the proton say to the electron?" He held back a chuckle. "Quit being so negative! Ha!" He snorted and slapped his knee. Emma didn't laugh. I managed a half-hearted guffaw, for Emma's sake.

"Hey, Lucas!" Keira said. "I heard you went to the doctor's and told him you wanted a little wart removed."

"Huh?" Lucas said.

"Yeah, so he had you thrown out of his office!" Keira chortled.

Lucas grimaced. I forced another laugh. Not a peep from Emma.

We were at the top of the track. Emma picked up her head from the bar and glanced down. She sucked in a sharp breath. Sweat rolled down her cheeks.

I looked over the edge and gasped.

The drop was so steep it was nearly vertical, plunging straight towards the churning sea.

My own stomach churned in response.

Forget smiling. I didn't see how any of us were even going to make it down this thing alive.

CHAPTER 8

Emma took several rapid breaths. Her whole body shook. The train creaked over the lip of the track. I had to do something. Fast. I racked my brains, trying to think of something, anything that would make her laugh.

Hang on . . .

I fumbled in Emma's pocket, brought out her camera phone, held it out in front of her, and with a shaky finger hit play.

I felt my stomach tip over as gravity snatched us.

"Just watch the screen, Emma," I told her. C'mon, c'mon . . .

Yes!

Keira's squealing face burst on screen, cheeks puffed out, eyes blinking rapidly as the camera panned back to reveal hundreds of rats swarming around her feet. Virtual Keira squealed again and did a crazy little dance like she was walking on hot lava.

"That's not funny!" the real Keira yelled.

"Yes, it is!" I said. The train thundered full-speed down the track. I could barely hold my head straight any more. I struggled to keep the video in front of Emma's face. She stared at it. "C'mon, Em!" I shook the phone and hit replay. Keira began her crazy dance again. Emma sucked in a deep breath. Then, despite herself, the edges of her mouth curled into a grin.

I looked up at a large camera perched above the tracks.

"Everyone smile!" I said.

I forced a grin as a click and flash went off above our heads. The train plummeted and the waves lurched up to meet us, then it suddenly swerved side-ways and we were shooting along above the water, slowing down. I breathed a long sigh of relief.

Keira threw her hands in the air.

"Woo-hoo! We made it!" she said.

"Lunatic," Lucas muttered.

I shook Emma's shoulders. "Good going, mate."

She nodded. Her lips were still trembling and her eyes were watering, but she wore a small, satisfied smile. "That was horrible," she said. "Now let's get off this thing."

The train rounded a bend and jerked to a stop back

in the station. The safety bar cranked open and we hopped out next to a GET YOUR PHOTOS HERE! booth. I was shocked to see the strange girl, Milly, standing behind the counter. But not as shocked as she was to see us.

"You made it!" she said, eyes wide, mouth even wider. She peeled a curling photo from a printer and pushed it across the counter. Lucas, Emma, Keira and I stared back from the grainy image – crazy-eyed, hair standing on end, knuckles white – but smiling. Well, Lucas's face was more of a mad grimace. But it would have to do.

"Whew!" I said. "We did it." Lucas and Emma high-fived.

But Keira's eyes narrowed as she leaned over the counter, glaring at Milly. She looked angry enough to grab the sword she still had in her belt.

"You knew what was in there, didn't you? 'Hey, how about riding Happy's Ghost Train?'" she said, imitating Milly's flat voice. "You get a kick out of tormenting people or something?" She lunged at Milly, but I managed to grab her by the shirt and pulled her back.

Emma rolled her eyes. "Yeah, you wouldn't know anything about tormenting people, would you now, Keira?" she said.

Keira huffed and continued to stare at Milly, who had started shaking from head to toe.

I reached over and put my hand on her thin shoulder.

"What's going on?" I asked.

Milly didn't answer, but I could feel her shoulder tense. She looked around nervously.

"It's OK. You can tell us," I said. "It's Happy, isn't it? Is he making you stay here?"

Milly nodded slightly and bit her trembling bottom lip.

Emma inspected Milly's face. "How long have you been here, anyway?" she said. "It looks like you haven't seen daylight in years."

Milly ignored the question. Her eyes flicked to a rat scrounging popcorn from a bin. "We can't talk here," she whispered. I glanced around. Weird. There wasn't a soul in sight.

Milly slipped from behind the photo counter and led us out of Happy's Ghost Train and down a deserted path.

"Where are we go—" Keira began.

"Shhh!" said Milly, walking faster. Finally, she stopped at a junction beneath a cluster of signs. One pointed down but read UP, another read EXIT and pointed to the sky, and a third read HAPPY'S FUNHOUSE but pointed both left and right. This place was giving me a headache.

Milly glanced around. Every path was empty. All I could see in the distance were the outlines of darkened rides and game booths. Keira planted her hands on her hips, nudging the sword in her belt.

"What is your problem, freak?" she said. "There's no one here. Are you mad or something?"

Milly placed a finger in front of her lips and leaned in closer.

"Look," she said. "I want to help you, OK?"

Keira rolled her eyes. "Sure," she muttered. "Like on that Ghost Train."

"I'm sorry," Milly whispered. "I didn't have a choice. But you made it! I didn't think you'd do that."

"Wow, thanks," I said.

Milly sucked in a breath. "It's just that no one has before."

"No one?" Emma said. She shot me a look. I shook my head, trying not to consider what that meant.

"No one," Milly repeated. "So maybe you have a chance."

"A chance?" I swallowed hard. "A chance of what?"

"Escape."

She looked over her shoulder again as if someone – or something – was watching her every move. "If you get through all three rides and defeat Happy, maybe he'll let you go." She cast a mournful glance into the distance, past the fence line and back into town. "Maybe he'll let all of us go." She started to inch away nervously, but I caught her arm.

"Wait!" I said. "Who are you?" She gave me a sad look and there was a flicker of something terribly

familiar in those pale blue eyes. Why couldn't I place it? Milly shook her head.

"Why are all these kids working in here so late at night?" I asked.

Milly didn't answer that, either. "Whatever you do," she said, "don't try to come out the way you came in. Once the gates close, the fences are electrified. And the only other way out is . . . that way." She pointed at the sea. Right. So it was getting fried alive or drowning in the dark. Some choice.

"Come on then," Keira said. "How are we supposed to escape?"

"You have to play his game . . . " she said. "And win."

A cold waft of sea air blew up the pathway, sending half-seen things skittering into the darkness. I could've sworn I heard the muffled moans and cries of children, but it might just have been the wind. Milly leaned in close again.

"Every ride is dangerous," she said. "But try Happy's Crazy Maze. It's probably the safest thing in the park."

Somehow, I had the feeling "safe" might be a bit of an overstatement. But we were going to have to take our chances.

"The maze it is," I said.

We inspected the signs above our heads. A crooked one painted with THE MAZE in mismatched letters pointed down the darkest of all three paths. Of course. Suddenly, the sign wobbled and fell sideways, creaking menacingly back and forth.

Lucas jumped.

"Ugh. I don't think I can take much more of this," he said.

"C'mon," Emma said, grabbing Lucas by the arm. "Let's just go and get it over with."

We started down the path but were interrupted by Milly's voice.

"Hold on!" she said. We turned to see her still standing at the junction, pale skin glowing in the moonlight. She tugged at the sleeves of her oversized Happyland uniform.

"Don't you want to hear a joke?" she said.

"A joke?" I said. "I don't think we're in the mood for—"

"No, you really want to hear this joke." She ran forward and grabbed me, wrapping her thin fingers around my arms, a desperate look in her eyes. "Trust me."

"'Trust me.' Sure," Keira mumbled under her breath.

I elbowed her. "OK," I said to Milly.

"How do you escape from a room with no doors, just a chair and a mirror on the wall?" Milly said.

"I don't know," I said.

"You look in the mirror and see what you saw," Milly replied. "Take the saw and cut the chair in half. Two halves make a whole. So climb through the hole and out of the room."

"That's it?" Keira said. "That wasn't funny. You're even more mental than Happy the Clown."

I ignored her. "What do you mean?" I asked Milly.

But she wasn't looking at us any more. She was staring in horror at something behind us. Her hand flew over her mouth.

"I've said too much," she whispered. "I'm going to be in terrible trouble." She hurried away, disappearing down the path behind a vacant game stall.

101

I searched everywhere to see what had fazed Milly. But all I spotted was a rat, perched on a signpost, chattering and nibbling its feet.

The mangy thing stared at us.

"Why is that rat . . . watching us?" Lucas said.

"I don't know," I said, yanking his arm. "Let's go."

We started walking, the rat still watching intently from its post. I picked up the pace, fighting the urge to run. It was just a stupid rat, after all.

Or was it?

I cast a quick glance back. The rat looked from side to side, kind of like the one back in the photo booth. Weird . . . Its beady red eyes flashed in the moonlight. Then it flicked its tail and scuttled away into the darkness.

CHAPTER 9

The maze took up the whole middle section of the pier, gnarly fake branches poking from five-metre-high plastic hedges. A bird had managed to fly directly into one of the hedges, ensnaring itself in the twisted mess; its skeleton with just a few frayed feathers still hung on it.

"*This* is supposed to be safe?" Lucas said. He shook his head. "I think I'll just wait out here."

"Oh no you won't, Pukas," Keira said. "You're

getting your picture taken. And you *will* smile!" She dragged him forward.

We walked through the entrance. Giant plastic bushes shaped like Happy the Clown's face grinned maniacally from either side. A sign dangled above, creaking on a single rusted chain:

> BEWARE THE TWISTED CRAZY MAZE,
> ALL YE WHO DARE RUSH IN!
> ONLY TO ROAM FOR DAYS AND DAYS,
> NEVER TO BE SEEN AGAIN!

That sounded really hopeful. Not.

Lo and behold, we hadn't made it three steps before a huge wall of plastic shrubbery blocked our way. Two paths extended in different directions, one to the left and one to the right.

"Which way?" Emma said.

"How about back the way we came?" Lucas said.

I ignored him. "This way," I said, turning left. It was fifty-fifty, after all. We hit another wall and went right. Then left. Then right. And left again. Lucas talked to himself the entire time.

"What are you doing, freak?" Keira said. "You're as mad as Milly!"

"Don't interrupt me!" Lucas said. "I'm remembering where we've gone. In case we need to find our way back." He began to chant his lefts and rights again.

"Nerd," Keira said.

"No, that's actually a good idea," I said. "Why don't we all keep track?"

Keira rolled her eyes, but Emma and I joined in repeating directions out loud. But after another dozen lefts and rights, we'd totally lost track. Then we hit a dead end.

"Left, right, right, right, left, left, right," Lucas said, rapid-fire. "No wait! It was left, right, right, left, left, left . . . oh no, I don't remember!" He slapped his forehead and ran his fingers through his tangle of hair. "This never would have happened if I still had my lucky hat! I've got to get out of here!" He started kicking the plastic shrubbery. There was a rustling sound and a rat carcass fell out. Keira winced, and Lucas jumped back, groaning. Emma put her hand on his shoulder.

"It's OK, mate," she said. "We're gonna get out of here. Isn't that right, Toby?"

"Sure," I said. But the truth was, I wasn't sure at all. The only thing I knew was if we didn't get out of here, we would die, probably of thirst or starvation. Like the rat.

And who would ever find us?

A cackle of electronic laughter came from behind us. We spun around. The hedges seemed to be moving.

"You have to be joking," Lucas said.

The hedge shifted once more and Happy the Clown emerged. Except not the real one. This one was made out of rustling green plastic leaves. It waved at us, red eyes flashing wickedly. We gasped.

"Hope you had a screaming good time on my Ghost Train!" it said in an electronic voice, then cackled again.

I reached in my pocket. "Yeah, we did," I said, shoving the picture in front of his face.

"Well look at that!" The red eyes flickered. "Smiles all around! You do look a bit green, though, young lady." He poked Emma's image. "Of course, that's

rather the pot calling the kettle black now, isn't it?" He chuckled. "Get it? Because I'm made of shrubbery! Sometimes I really crack myself up!"

None of us said a word. We definitely didn't laugh.

"Don't worry," the Happy-shrub said. "You'll have just as much fun in here. It's a real rip-roaring time. Just don't get lost. Oh, and watch out for the lions!"

"The what?" Keira said.

"Just my little joke," Happy chuckled. "You know I do love a good joke! Have fun now!" He swung a topiary arm above his head and spun to leave.

"Wait!" I said. "As it happens, we are a little lost. How about a clue?"

"Why, of course! This is Happyland, where the fun never, ever, ever ends!" he cackled. "Let's see now. It's quite simple, really. All you need to do is take the first left . . . "

"OK," I said.

"Then third right,"

I nodded.

"Then second left, first left, fifth left, third right ..."
Happy sped up, until he was rattling off directions so
quickly I thought his leafy head might pop off.
Unfortunately, I was lost somewhere back on the
second left. Or was it third right?

"Hehe! Easy, right? Or is it left?" Happy giggled.

"Wait, I—"

"Very well, then, cheerio!" Happy said with a wave
and backed away. A hedge slid across, and he was gone.

"Wonderful," Keira grumbled. "Did you get all that,
boy genius?" She poked Lucas.

He shook his head in defeat.

"Me neither," I said. It looked like we really were
going to be lost in here for ever.

"No worries," Emma said with a grin. "I did!"

She held up her phone and hit play, and Happy's instructions echoed back at us. She must have been filming the whole time!

"Nice job!" Keira said.

"Um . . . thanks. I don't know why I didn't think of it earlier," Emma answered in a high voice, clearly surprised. I was surprised, too. For some reason, Keira didn't seem so bad in Happyland. But maybe it was just because she was right at home here with all the lunatics.

We crunched across the gravel paths, following Happy's instructions back through the maze. Left. Right. Left. Left. Left. I rubbed my head. I was getting dizzy and disoriented. We had to be out of here soon. It felt like we'd walked miles.

The Happy recording sped through three more

turns and stopped. Emma tapped pause, rewound the video and hit replay. "Almost there," she said.

"Whew," Lucas sighed. "This wasn't nearly as bad as I expected."

And that was when the low growl came from around the corner.

"What was that, Toby?" Lucas said. "You hungry or something?"

The growling grew louder. And closer.

"No," I said with a gulp, "but I think someone else is."

A head popped round the corner. An actual, real, live lion, head down low, growling. It looked like it had escaped from the circus – about ten years ago. Its big sparkly ruff was torn and faded. Its claws were long and jagged. I could see the outline of its ribs beneath its matted fur. The lion pawed the ground, shook its ratty mane and snarled, baring sharp yellow teeth.

I wondered if it was too late to take the roller coaster again.

CHAPTER 10

Lucas, Emma and I linked arms and inched slowly back.

"There's no place like home, there's no place like home," Lucas chanted, eyes closed.

"Yeah, OK. You wait for the wonderful Wizard of Oz." Keira reached for her belt and whipped out the sword from Happy's Ghost Train. "Meanwhile I'll sort this out!"

She stepped forward, brandished the sword high above her head and smacked it on to the ground.

"Bad kitty!" she yelled. Lucas, Emma and I jumped.

The lion didn't even flinch. It just sunk its head lower, let out another low growl and crept forward, never taking its eyes off its prey. Us. All I could picture was the ferocious, drooling beast I once saw on some wildlife programme chasing a herd of defenceless zebras across the savannah. Only this was way worse. Because we were the zebras.

"Keira," I whispered. "Forget it. We've got to go back!"

"No way," Keira said in a snarl almost as low as the lion's. "We're almost there. I'm not turning around now!"

The lion bared its teeth. Drool fell from the edges of its mouth. It shook its head and roared.

"Keira!" I said. "Don't be stupid!"

She spun around. "I said, *I AM NOT GOING BACK!*"

With that, she raised her sword and hacked into the plastic shrubbery, carving a new path. For once, Keira was actually being pretty smart. I kept one eye on the growling lion as Emma, Lucas and I reached in and pulled mangled leaves out of the way. Finally, there was enough room to squeeze through. The lion watched us push our way to the other side. I breathed a sigh of relief.

"That was close," Emma said.

"A bit too clo . . . " Lucas began, then his eyes flew wide. "Noooooooo!" he screamed just as the lion leapt through the hedge with a mighty roar.

"Run!" I yelled.

We pelted down pathway after pathway. Left or right didn't matter, as long as it was away from the lion. I could practically feel its hot breath on my neck. We ran faster, skidding around a corner. The lion skidded after us, never more than a bend behind. I didn't know how long we could keep this up.

Suddenly, Lucas slowed.

"C'mon, mate!" I grabbed Lucas's arm. "Don't stop now!"

"No," he said, shaking me free. "Just wait a minute!"

The lion rounded the corner, its black eyes glinting.

"I'd really rather not!" I said.

The lion crept forward, a low-tone rumbling coming from its mouth. Lucas scrabbled in his backpack, tossing comics, tissues and Maths textbooks to the ground. Wonderful. What was he going to do? Blast the thing with his inhaler?

"Aha!" he yelled. "Got it!" He held a squashed ham

sandwich wrapped in cling film triumphantly over his head. "Mum packed it in case I got hungry."

"Fine time for a snack, weirdo," Keira muttered.

Lucas picked the wrapper off the sandwich and quickly chucked it over the lion's growling head. I watched in awe as the sandwich sailed through the air, disappearing somewhere deep in the hedges. It was the furthest I'd seen Lucas throw anything. Ever. Mr McNulty, our PE teacher, would have fainted in shock. The lion lifted its head, sniffed the air, turned and ran after it.

"Yes!" Lucas said.

We wasted no time celebrating. Feet pounding, we raced in the opposite direction, dodging around corners until we were sure we'd lost the beast. Finally, we stopped, gasping for breath. I leaned over on my knees and raised one hand in the air.

"Good one, Lucas!" I panted. We high-fived.

"Yeah, not bad, Pukas," said Keira. "But where are we?"

My heart sank as I looked up and down the twisting paths. Every direction looked just the same.

"Great," Lucas said. "We're stuck in here." He slumped to the ground. "And we don't even have a sandwich any more."

I looked at my best friend, shoulders hunched, head down. "No," I said. "No way are we going to be stuck in here!"

I could only think of one thing to do. It was a long shot, but I didn't care.

"Cover your ears, guys," I said.

Emma, Keira and Lucas shot me confused looks but put their hands over their ears.

I stuck my fingers in my mouth and let out a terrific

whistle. If there's one thing I'm good at, it's whistling. Not much of a skill, but I was hoping this time it might be just what we needed. At first, nothing happened. I whistled again. Louder. Maybe one of the creepy fairground kids would give us a hand.

Yes! This time, a distant whistle came in response.

Emma raised an eyebrow. "What was that?" she said. The whistle sounded once more.

"Our way out of here," I said. "We need to follow the sound."

Emma shook her head. "I don't know, Toby. It could be a trap."

"Well, what other choice do we have?" I said. "Should we just sit here and wait for the lion to come back?"

Emma shrugged. "I still don't like it," she said. "What if it's Happy?"

The stranger whistled again.

"We have to hope it's one of the kids," I said. "Helping us."

Lucas groaned. "Yeah, because everyone here has been sooooo helpful," he said.

"Well, I don't care if it's Santa Claus or the Big Bad Wolf," Keira said. "I am not going to wait around here doing nothing! A lion doesn't take long to eat a sandwich."

She raised her sword and began chopping a path straight towards the sound. Lucas, Emma and I followed, squeezing our way between rows and rows of clumped-together hedges. By the time we stumbled into the centre of the maze my legs and arms were covered with dozens of scratches.

We ended up in a run-down courtyard. Empty food containers and ripped-up tickets littered the plastic

lawn. A giant statue of Happy the Clown rose tall in the centre, tangled in fake weeds.

And standing at the base, mouth curled in a whistle, was Milly. She tugged nervously at her Happyland uniform and half-smiled.

"You!" Keira said, shocked. "Why are you helping us?"

Milly's mouth opened. But before she could answer, a shadow fell over her. The topiary Happy emerged from behind the statue. And this time, he was wielding a giant pair of garden shears.

"Because she's a very naughty girl," he said with a cackle. He snapped the shears just centimetres from Milly's terrified face. "As for the rest of you ... congratulations! You made the cut!" He lowered the shears and lunged straight at us.

"Oh no you don't, you overgrown salad!" Keira

yelled. She swung her sword, lopping off one of Happy's hedge arms. The giant bush simply dropped his weapon and kept coming at us, laughing. I dodged past and grabbed the shears. They were way heavier than I expected. My arms ached. I grunted, heaved the metal blades in the air and with one jerky swing took Happy's leafy head right off.

It tumbled across the ground.

Still laughing.

I'd had just about enough of this place. "Let's go!" I said, dropping the shears.

I grabbed Milly and we all raced towards the exit, following the narrow path that ran straight to the other side of the maze.

"Don't forget to say cheese!" The cackling Happy head yelled behind us.

Right. We looked up at the camera perched on the

gatepost above our heads, managing smiles just before the flash and the click. We ran breathlessly out of the gate and skidded to a stop on the other side. Two down, one to go ... I looked around for another photo booth. There wasn't one. Terrific. How were we supposed to get out of here without our picture?

"OK, now what?" Emma said. She looked to Milly. The pale girl just shook her head.

"I can't," she said shakily. "I'd better be going. Before, before ... oh, no!" She gasped.

A swarm of rats quickly surrounded our feet, crawling up the hedges and signposts, covering every spare bit of ground. Keira's sword clattered from her hands.

"No, no, no," she said, covering her eyes.

"Keira!" I shook her by the shoulder. "Get a hold of yourself! You faced a lion and didn't even flinch! It's

just a bunch of little rodents. They can't do anything to you, OK?"

Keira straightened up a little, peeked through her fingers and nodded her head. "OK," she said. Although she didn't sound totally convinced.

A rustling sound came from the maze. I spun around to see the topiary Happy, cradling the laughing head in its remaining arm. I grabbed the sword, ready to chop the stupid thing to bits if necessary. But it didn't attack. Instead, it leaned forward and bowed. The laughing came to a stop, replaced by the sound of wheels clacking. What on earth? Lucas tugged my arm and pointed.

A miniature carriage rolled up the pathway. Like everything else in Happyland, it looked like it had once been fancy. But now, the black paint had faded to a dull grey, the gold trim chipped and gashed. The rusted wheels squealed. A small army of rats in harnesses and tiny top hats strained to pull it forward. And on the faded red driver's seat sat Happy the Clown, the real Happy, grinning as usual, with a rat perched on his shoulder.

He shook the reins and the rats halted.

"Well, well, well," he said. "It looks like congratulations are in order!" But he didn't exactly sound pleased. In fact, his wild orange hair looked even more dishevelled than earlier and his black eye make-up ran in streaks down his white-painted face. A rat clambered down the side of the rusted carriage and joined the minions swarming around our feet. I shuddered.

Happy extended a gloved hand and shook a glossy photo in my face. I reached out, but before I could grab hold he let go. The picture fluttered to the ground.

"Gotcha!" he chuckled.

I scooped the picture from the top of a pile of squirming rats and flipped it over. We were smiling. All of us. *Yes!*

"Yeah," I said with a satisfied grin, shaking the photo back at Happy. "But not for long."

And for once, Happy didn't smile.

CHAPTER 11

The clown nodded at the picture in my hand. "OK, so it looks like you enjoyed the maze after all," he said. "Meet any big kitties in there? See, I wasn't lion. Get it? Lion. L-I-O-N! Hahahahahahahahahahahaha!" he cackled maniacally and slapped his knee. "Meeeeoooowwwww!"

Then suddenly he sat up straight. The corners of his red-painted mouth twisted down.

"Now," he said, "I know that naughty girl Milly

helped you." He stroked the rat perched on his shoulder. "My little friends keep me informed of everything that goes on in the park. *Everything*." He pulled a piece of mouldy cheese from his pocket, fed it to the rodent and narrowed his eyes. "But don't worry, we only reward the good children around here. The bad children . . . well, we have ways of dealing with them too."

Happy let out a low whistle and the scuttling rats swarmed all over Milly, knocking her down and lifting her off her feet. She let out an ear-piercing wail. I reached out to grab her, but all I caught was the corner of her Happyland shirt. It slipped between my fingers.

"No!" I yelled.

I watched in horror as the rats whisked her down the path and away into the darkness. Keira choked back a scream. Milly's muffled cries faded, until all we

could hear was Happy's demonic laugher. "Where are they taking her?" I demanded.

Happy smiled a creepy smile. "Why, to my Funhouse, of course," he said. "To be taught a lesson! So I can stop her ruining everyone else's fun. Stop her for good."

"You're mad!" Emma blurted out. Happy's black-painted eyebrows shot up, and she sank back and grabbed my arm.

"I suppose I probably am," he said. He stuck two fingers in his mouth and delivered a high-pitched whistle like the one the robot made in the Ghost Train, but with a different note sequence. In a flash, the rats scurried away.

"One more photo, and then you're free," said Happy. "Ta-ra!" He shook the reins and his carriage lurched forward, the team of rats straining once more

against their tiny harnesses. "Have a good time now!" Happy called back. "Make sure to enjoy your *last ride!*" His laughter faded as he disappeared into the night.

"Wh-wh-what did that mean? 'Last ride'?" Lucas said.

"Who cares?" Keira snorted in response. "Let's just get it over with and get out of here!" She glanced around her feet as if to make sure no more rats were squirming about.

"Maybe they've got a kiddie ride around here somewhere," Emma said. "You know, like enchanted tea cups or something. We need to find a map . . . " She began down a path.

I stayed put. "No," I said. "We need to find Milly."

The other stared at me like I was as crazy as Happy the Clown.

"What?" Keira said. "You've got to be joking!"

I thought about Happy's Funhouse, perched at the end of the pier, surrounded by nothing but churning waves. I kind of wished I *was* joking. "No, I'm not," I said. "We need to help her."

"I don't know," Emma said. "She's the one who got us on that Ghost Train in the first place."

"Maybe she didn't have a choice!" I said. "Look, it's not exactly like I'm dying to go there, either."

Lucas shuddered.

"OK," I said. "Bad choice of words. You know what I mean. But we've got to do *something*."

"You know, Keira and Emma may have a point," Lucas chimed in. "Plus, we still need that third photo . . . "

"But what about Milly? And the other kids?" I said. "Maybe Happy has got them trapped. Who knows

how long they've been here?" I thought of the boy at the popcorn stand. Twenty years he'd said he'd been working for. Maybe it was actually true.

"Well, I definitely don't want to be here any longer than I have to," Keira said. "Let's just get that photo. Then maybe we can figure something out ..." She hesitated.

All I could picture was Milly, her pale haunted figure, and that terrified look in her eyes as the rats carried her away.

"Oh, forget it!" I said. "If you won't help me, I'll just have to do it myself."

I hefted the sword and marched off in the direction of the Funhouse. The signs took me back through the deserted main avenue and beside the sea. I shivered as I passed the empty food and game stalls. There was not a soul in sight. Not a seagull. Not a rat. Nothing. Still, I could've sworn I heard voices whispering, *"To-by! To-beeeee!"* over the sound of churning waves.

I walked as fast as I could and tried not the think about what was waiting for me at the end of this twisted path. I tried not to think about the fact my so-called friends had just ditched me. I tried to forget this was the worst birthday. Ever.

I began to wonder if I'd live to see another one . . .

Finally, I reached the path to Happy's Funhouse at the end of the pier. Waves crashed on either side. Black lamp posts ran the entire length, casting dim triangles of light on the old wood. The dark outline of a big top loomed at the end, stretching the full width of the pier and blotting out the low-hanging moon.

In front of it was a colourful wooden construction – Happy's Funhouse.

Yeah, right. By now, I was pretty sure that nothing in Happyland lived up to its name.

A terrible wind howled along the pier, shaking the lamps and setting the big top's canvas walls flapping. I sucked in a breath of salt air and gulped. Maybe this wasn't such a great idea. Maybe I never should have come here on my own. But the churning waves urged me on.

"To-by! To-beeee!"

I glanced over my shoulder. The dim lights of Weirville flickered in the distance. My heart sank. I wondered if I'd ever make it home. I wondered if I'd ever see Mum again. Or Dad. Or my pet fish. And to think I was so worried about my stupid football. Happy could keep it, for all I cared.

I squared my shoulders and gripped the sword a little tighter. The only thing to do now was go forward. I took a shaky step up the path. The wood of the pier creaked beneath my feet. It felt like I had a million more steps to go . . .

"Hold up!" a voice said from behind.

I turned around. Emma, Lucas and Keira were racing towards me.

"Hey." Emma punched my shoulder playfully. "You ran away quickly back there!"

"Don't you remember?" Lucas added. "We stick together, right?"

"Yeah, *together*, wimp," Keira said.

I smiled. "Right. Thanks, guys."

Side by side, we continued along the old pier. As we did, dozens of kids in Happyland uniforms emerged from the darkness, pale faces shining beneath the lamp posts. They all wore the same blank expressions, eyes wide and hollow. They watched our every step, unblinking.

"What do they want?" Lucas said, cowering.

"Don't go!" they answered in monotone voices. "Turn around!"

We kept walking, trying to ignore them. But more and more children emerged, forming an ominous chant along the edge of the pier.

"Don't be foolish!" they said.

"Get out now!"

"While you still can!"

"Don't end up like us!"

"Turn back, turn back, turn back ... "

Finally, we stopped.

"Who are you?" Emma asked.

The blank-eyed children had no answer.

"What are you doing here?" I said. They just stared in response, shaking their heads, pale arms hanging limply from their oversized uniforms.

"I don't know about you lot," Keira said. "But I really don't want to hang around to find out."

We broke into a run, but skidded to a halt at the end of the pier and looked up at Happy's lair. It was even more terrifying up close, with a lopsided HAPPY'S FUNHOUSE sign hanging over the entrance, the faded remnants of Happy's grinning face standing in for the 'O'. Beyond loomed the big top, with faded red, green and blue banners hanging in tatters from the tall posts. From the centre of the roof rose a cluster of antennae and a huge Happy the Clown statue, cranking in slow circles, eyes wobbling unnaturally back and forth in its head. "Oh, God. Do we really have to go in here?" Lucas said.

137

"It's OK," I said. "I'll go first. Just stay behind me."

I took a deep breath, gripped the sword and creaked up the front steps. A revolving glass door spun slowly in front of me. I looked back at the faces of my friends, nodded and took one cautious step forward. But as soon as my foot crossed the line, the door sucked me in completely. It spun faster. And faster. Until finally, it spat me out on the other side. Dizzy. Confused.

And completely alone.

"Hello?" I said.

No one answered.

"Lucas? Emma? Keira?"

Silence.

I tucked the sword under my arm, wiped my sweaty palms on my knees and looked around. I was standing in a hall of mirrors. Hundreds of versions of me looked back. I saw myself from every angle – side on, front on, the back of my head. I turned to find the door, but somehow it wasn't there any more, and instead I just found myself up against another mirror and my own scared face. I searched the tiny room. No exit in sight. I began to hyperventilate. *No, no, no!* I screwed my eyes shut, trying to convince myself this wasn't like the time I got locked in the cellar when I was five.

Yeah, I get claustrophobic. Really, properly claustrophobic.

I slowly opened my eyes and took in the tiny room once more.

This was so much worse than the cellar when I was five.

"Help," I croaked.

But I could barely breathe, let alone yell. The mirrors seemed to shift, slowly hemming me in to a

tighter and tighter spot. My claustrophobia kicked up a notch and all the moisture seemed to leave my throat. I put my hands to my temples, trying to control my spinning head. Something flitted past in the mirror in front of me. Something orange, white and red.

Happy?

I spun around. The room was empty. Except for a statue of Happy standing in the centre, elbow propped on an old wooden chair. The statue smiled serenely. But I swore I could see the evil glinting in its stone eyes, the mocking in its toothless grin.

I had to get out of here. Now. I reached my free hand out in front of me, feeling along every surface, trying to find a way out. My sweaty palms slid across the glass. My vision blurred. My heart raced. Mirrors. Mirrors. And more mirrors.

And a thousand ghost-faced Tobys staring back at me in fear.

I fell to the floor, shaking.

I was never getting out of here.

CHAPTER 12

I tucked my knees beneath my chin, taking deep breaths. I had to stay calm. *Breathe in, breathe out.* Mum always said to inhale and exhale in a steady rhythm when I was stressed. *In. Out.* Slowly, I started to relax. I closed my eyes and pictured Mum's face. Her hand on my back. And then, oddly, her features began to morph in my mind's eye. They grew smaller. Younger. Similar, yet different somehow . . .

Milly!

The image in my mind spoke:

"Look in the mirror and see what you saw. Take the saw and cut the chair in half. Two halves make a whole. So climb through the hole and out of the room."

I jumped to my feet. A clue! That wasn't a joke after all; Milly was giving us a clue. I looked into the nearest mirror ... *and see what you saw.* But no saw appeared. It was just me, the chair and that creepy Happy statue. And in my hand ... Of course. The sword!

I lifted the blade high in the air with both hands and swung it down hard over the chair. The wood splintered. The chair split easily into two halves. There was a pause, then a creak as a section of the floor below slid away to reveal a trapdoor leading to darkness.

I didn't think. I just crouched, grabbed the edges of the floor and lowered myself through. My feet dangled

143

into nothing. What choice did I have? I let go and landed on something hard, then I was sliding.

I shot out into the light, and just as I saw a camera flash, I managed to smile. There was the whirr of a printer somewhere in the darkness above me.

I found myself at the bottom of a Funhouse slide, and looked up to see Emma, Lucas and Keira staring at me.

"Where have you been?" Emma said, hands on her hips. "You scared us half to death disappearing like that!"

"Yeah, we were supposed to stick together, remember?" Lucas said, pointing his finger accusingly. "You said so!"

"I know," I said. "That door, it just sucked me in. And all the mirrors. And the tiny room . . . " It was too awful to talk about.

144

Something floated down and landed in my hands. A photo of me, smiling.

Keira reached over and snatched the picture from my hands. "I'll have that," she said.

"Seriously, Keira?" I rolled my eyes. I'd pretty much had enough of her by now. "What do you want with my picture? Gonna draw a fake moustache on it and post it on the wall at school?"

Keira narrowed her eyes at me. I narrowed mine back.

"We agreed to save Milly, remember?" I said.

Keira nodded. "That's right," she said, pulling out all the photos and fanning them in front of me. "And this is our best shot at saving ourselves, and rescuing Milly, *and* all the other kids!"

I'm pretty sure my jaw hit the ground. "Uh, yeah ... " I stammered.

"Oh, just stop burbling and come on!" Keira said. She jammed the pictures into her pocket. "We've got to find Happy!"

I climbed from the slide. We were now in a courtyard separating the Funhouse from the big top. Only it wasn't much of a garden any more. Dead plants and flowers with their blooms lopped off clustered around decaying benches. Weeds poked through the slats of the wooden pier. Murky water trickled out of a cracked fountain. Above, we could see the stars.

"Where do we go?" Emma said.

Without a word, Lucas raised a shaking finger and pointed to a sign above our heads:

Happy's Tea Party – join the party with everyone's favourite clown!

A crooked arrow pointed into the big top.

"Good job, Pukas!" Keira slapped him on the back. Lucas gulped. For a moment, he looked like he might live up to his nickname. Then he squared his shoulders.

"It's *Lu*-cas," he said with emphasis. "L for Lima! Or lame, or loser. Whatever you prefer. Got it? Unless you want me to start calling you ... "

Keira put her hands on her hips and raised an eyebrow. Lucas looked back and forth.

"Whiskers!" he said. The corners of his lips twitched into a smile. He put two fingers to his mouth and made chattering rat noises.

Keira lifted a hand. Lucas sunk back in his heels and raised two bony fists in response. Uh-oh. This wasn't going to be pretty. But then, Keira grinned. Her hand landed on Lucas's shoulder in a friendly thump. Lucas wobbled back and forth, shocked, but wearing a satisfied smile on his face.

"Yeah, OK, I got it," Keira said. "Now let's get moving, *Lucas*!"

We followed the signs down a pathway and into the big top tent. Whenever the wind blew outside, the faded red, green and blue canvas walls shook and strained against their supports. A huge structure rose from the middle, top slowly spinning. What was that thing? Then, I remembered with a shudder: the Happy the Clown statue with all the weird antennae clustered beside it.

Keira pushed aside the tent flap, and we all crept through. I just hoped this wasn't where that lion had escaped from . . .

Inside, the big top was cavernous, but nearly empty – just a large dirt floor, and a platform right in

the middle. On the platform there was a neatly laid table and chairs, together with a shabby sideboard and cupboards, as though it were an old-fashioned drawing room.

The tea party.

Emma stopped in her tracks. "Whoa . . . " she said. I watched as her wide eyes followed the scaffolding along the sides of the big top all the way to the highest point.

"Don't worry, Em," I said. "It's not like you have to go up there or anything!"

She shuddered and we started walking again until we reached the steps up to the platform. A tattered red velvet rope hung across the steps next to a sign that read:

HAPPY'S TEA PARTY
PROPER ATTIRE REQUIRED

"Here goes nothing," I said. I unlatched the rope. It dropped to the ground, sending up a puff of dust and wood chips. Emma, Lucas, Keira and I looked at each other, nodded and slowly climbed the steps on to the platform.

No sooner had we walked in than a trapdoor opened ahead and Happy leapt up out of it, orange hair flying, red eyes wild. We screamed as one and jumped back a step. Happy laughed and ran up and down, slapping party hats on each of our stunned heads.

"Now *that's* proper party-wear!" he said, rubbing his oversized gloves together.

"What is *wrong* with you?" Emma shrieked.

"Why, I just want everyone to be happy here at Happyland!" His mouth twisted into a lopsided smirk. He placed a party hat on his own head, elaborately snapping the elastic beneath his chin. "Ooh! That tickles!" he giggled.

"Now ... do you have all of your smiley happy photos?" He held out a hand and waggled his fingers.

Keira pulled out the pictures.

I caught her arm. "Hold on a minute," I said. "Where's Milly?" I asked Happy. "How about you let her go first? Then we can talk about the pictures."

"Oh dear me, no," Happy said. "I'd love to, but little Miss Milly has been a very naughty girl. I'm afraid she's rather tied up right now!"

"What is that supposed to mean?" I said.

Happy kicked open one of the shabby cupboards. Inside, Milly sat bound to a chair, gagged, her arms twisted around her body in a straitjacket. She shook her head violently. Tears squeezed from the corners of her eyes.

"Behold!" Happy said. "The Terrible Houdini! *Terrible*, get it? Because she can't escape!"

He slammed the door shut. I could hear Milly's muffled cries from behind the rotting wood.

"You can't keep her locked up in there!" Emma said, shaking.

"Actually, I can," Happy said, with a grin. "But don't worry. She won't be lonely. Now that you kids are here, you can keep her company . . . *for ever*!" He cackled.

"But what about the pictures?" Emma snatched the photos from Keira's hand and shoved them in front of Happy. "Here! You can have them. Now, let us go. You promised!"

Happy took the photos, giggled and chucked them over his shoulder. They fluttered to the ground. "Don't be silly," he said. "That was just a joke!"

We stared at him in disbelief. He looked back and forth between each of us.

"What?" he said. "Why aren't you laughing? Aren't I funny?"

We slowly began to back away.

"You're about as funny as a funeral!" Keira blurted out.

Happy smiled. "Oh, you flatter me, dear!" he said. "Please, do join me!" He nodded over his shoulder to the table.

We carried on inching away. Happy put his hands on his hips.

"Tsk, tsk," he said. "Children are so rude these days! No manners whatsoever! Have a seat! I insist! Wouldn't want to have to make an example of your little friend now, would I?" He glanced at Milly's cupboard and smirked.

153

"I don't know what that means, but we can't leave her here," I whispered. "We've got to do as he says."

Lucas, Emma and Keira just nodded. We followed Happy across the platform, to the table.

I settled into a small, red chair that must have been designed for a three year old. It was hard to stay upright on the puny thing. Emma, Keira and Lucas carefully lowered themselves into the miniature chairs alongside mine.

Happy sat opposite us. The table was all laid out with tea, cups, saucers and fancy little cakes. I'm pretty sure Lucas's stomach actually grumbled. I shot him a look.

"What?" he said under his breath. "The lion ate my sandwich!"

Happy clapped his hands together. "Lovely, lovely!" he said. He leaned to one side and pulled a lever I hadn't seen. At once, the platform around us fell away, leaving us and the table stranded on an island. I leaned back in my seat, and saw a huge net filled with colourful balls dangling at least ten metres below. And beneath that – the churning sea. We were perched right on the edge. Emma recoiled and shrieked.

"Don't worry, young lady! I promise, you'll have a ball!" Happy chortled. "Now, this is my Funhouse. Let's have some FUN!"

He grinned widely, baring his pointy yellow teeth. Emma sank back in her chair.

"What do you want from us, anyway?" she said.

"Why nothing, dear," Happy said, shifting his teacup around on the saucer.

"Right," I said.

"You don't believe me?" he said.

"No. I think I know what you're up to," I said.

Happy raised a black-painted eyebrow.

"I think you lure kids to the park," I continued. "Then you keep them here for ever, right?"

Happy shook his head. "No, that's not right at all," he said. "Now, would you dislike a cup of tea?"

"No," I said. "I don't want any tea! I just want to get out of here!"

"Very well, then," Happy said. And poured me a cup of tea.

"What are you doing?" I asked. "I just said I don't want any tea."

"Oh," Happy said, sliding the cup and saucer in front of me. "I thought you knew! This is a backwards tea party. You have to say the opposite of what you mean! Am I not clever?"

"No, you are not," I said.

Happy grinned. "Thank you, young man."

I pushed the tea away.

"So, tell me," I said. "Does that mean you are *not* the reason my aunt went missing twenty-five years ago?"

"Why, of course not!" Happy said with a big smile. "Nothing to do with me!"

My stomach lurched. I looked back across the gap towards the cupboard where Milly was trapped.

"Please, then," I said. "Will you never let us out?"

Happy lifted his teacup and took a dainty sip, pinky pointing in the air. Then he slammed the cup back on the saucer. Tea sloshed from the sides and he gave a wicked grin.

"Absolutely."

CHAPTER 13

Happy lifted the teapot and sloppily splashed tea into the remaining cups. Keira scoffed.

"I'd rather drink petrol," she said, pushing the cup away with a haughty little sniff. "I don't do tea with lunatics!"

"Surely you don't mean that!" Happy said.

"Yeah, I surely do!" Keira shot back.

"Keira!" I shook my head at her. Her eyes widened as she realised her mistake. Happy grinned and pushed a button.

The floor dropped out below Keira's chair and she fell, screaming, into the ball pit below.

"Hope you enjoy my Super-Happy-Fun Ball Pool!" Happy said with a cackle. "It's a real lively place!"

Keira squirmed. I watched in horror as dozens of bones began popping up among the brightly coloured balls. She knocked away a skull and shrieked.

"Let me out of here!" she wailed, arms and legs flailing. She tried to pull herself up, but couldn't right herself because of the balls. Happy peeked his orange head over the edge and laughed again.

"Why I'd be glad to!" he called back.

"Anyone else not care to join her?" He glanced around the table and fixed his red-eyed stare on Lucas. "Perhaps you, young man?"

Lucas looked down his nose at Keira wiggling

helplessly among the balls and bones. "Uh, no thanks," he said, then stopped short. "Oh, no . . ."

Happy twirled his oversized index finger in the air and poked the button. "See you soon!" he said with a wave.

Lucas screamed as his chair dumped him into the ball pit.

"I'll get you for this!" he yelled.

"Hahaha! Certainly you will!" Happy answered, then turned his attention back to Emma and me.

"And how about you, Miss?" Happy nodded towards the pit.

"Yes, please," she said shakily. "I'd like to join my friends now." She closed her eyes and gripped the sides of the chair. Happy twirled his finger in the air . . . then picked up a little cake and popped it in his mouth.

"Quite delicious!" he said, spitting frosting and cake pieces on to his plate. "Like they were just baked today! I insist you don't try one." He shoved the cakes in my direction. I picked one up. It was hard as a rock. Happy eyed me. I said nothing, just put the edge of the stale cake in my mouth, took a small nibble and set it back down again.

Happy began peppering us with questions. I had to think of a plan. Soon. It was just a matter of time before one of us slipped up and landed in the net below. Or both of us. Then there would be nobody left to do the rescuing and we might really be trapped here for ever.

There was only one thing for it. I'd just have to beat him at his own game.

I took a deep breath, figuring it all out in my head before I spoke. "Happy," I said at last. "Will you not

ever promise not to never do the opposite of not letting us out?"

"Yes!" he said.

I grinned and set my cup down.

"I mean, no!" Happy shook his head, crazy orange hair shooting in every direction. "Wait!" he yelled. "What did you say?"

I shrugged.

Happy leapt to his feet. "That's cheating!" he said.

"And you wouldn't know a thing about cheating now, would you?" I said with a grin. Emma reached over and poked the button in front of Happy's chair.

The floor below him fell away, and Happy tumbled down, screaming the entire way and landing with a splash of balls – right next to Keira and Lucas.

"Uh-oh," Emma said.

Happy scrambled towards Lucas and grabbed him by the throat. Lucas squeaked and tried to wriggle away, but without any luck. Keira swiftly raised a combat boot.

"Hands off my mate, you big clown!" she yelled. And with that, she kicked Happy away like a football. Impressive. Maybe Keira had a shot at being goalkeeper this year ...

Happy landed upside down on the other side of the ball pit. He tried in vain to right himself, but all his squirming weight was too much for the rotting net. There was a snapping sound as the strands started to give way beneath him.

"You'll be sorry ..." he yelled. "I'll—"

His words became a howling cry as he slipped through the torn net, tumbling down to the sea in an avalanche of balls. The waves swallowed him.

Keira and Lucas grabbed the net and clung on for dear life.

"Told you I don't do tea with lunatics!" Keira yelled.

Emma and I jumped up. We looked down at Lucas and Keira, still trapped six metres below amid the tangle of netting.

"Any chance of a hand?" Lucas called up.

"How are we going to get them out of there?" I said. "I don't know how long that net will hold."

Emma glanced around the tent, then up.

"I think I have an idea," she said, biting her lower lip. "Why don't you take care of her ... " She tilted her head at Milly's cupboard. "I'll get something for them." She pointed at the pit and then took off towards the side of the big top.

I ran to the cupboard and flung open the door,

pulling the gag from Milly's mouth. She let out a huge breath.

"Thank you," she said. "I thought I was going to be stuck in here for ever!"

I slid the chair out, undid the ties and released Milly from the straitjacket. She shook her arms and glanced nervously around the platform.

"Where's Happy?" she said.

"Taking a swim." I pointed to the ball pit.

For the first time, Milly actually smiled.

"C'mon," she said, grabbing my hand. "We don't have much time. It'll be morning soon. Then it will be too late."

"Too late for what?" I said.

"Just follow me."

She walked swiftly to the side of the big top and flung open a tent flap. Beyond was a small room with

dozens of electrical panels and television screens lining the walls. A chair sat in the middle beneath a single light bulb dangling from an extension cord. I raised an eyebrow at Milly.

"It's the control room," she said, "for the whole park." She pulled my arm, leading me to a button marked TURNSTILES. She pointed a shaking finger at it.

"That one?" I said.

Milly nodded.

I reached out and pushed it.

There was a crackle of electricity and the security monitors overhead lit up. I jumped back a step. The screen filled with grainy black-and-white images of children – hundreds of them – flooding through the unlocked turnstiles and out of the park. They streamed silently into the night, until all that was left was the Happy the Clown statue at the entrance, arm swinging up and down in some sort of freaky salute goodbye.

Then, the screens went dark.

Milly put her hand over her mouth and gasped.

"I can't believe it," she said. "You did it!"

"We did it," I answered.

Milly choked back tears. "I guess I should be going now, too," she said and cast her eyes downward. Those blue eyes. Those very, very familiar blue eyes.

I knew exactly where I'd seen them before.

"I worked it out," I told her.

"Worked *what* out?" she asked.

"Who you are."

Milly tilted her head to the side. Her left pigtail brushed her shoulder. Just like that tiny black and white picture Mum kept on the mantelpiece. The one of Mum and her sister at the beach. On the morning of her eleventh birthday.

"Milly is short for Camille, isn't it?" I said.

Milly nodded.

"And you went missing twenty-five years ago, right?" Milly kept nodding. "And you have a sister named Harriet. Harriet Parker, right?"

A tear rolled down her cheek. "Yes," she whispered. "Harrie. I've missed her so much."

"Harriet's my mum," I said.

Milly just stared at me. "Your mum?" she said, shaking her head. "Little Harrie has *kids*?"

I nodded. "Yeah," I said. "So I guess that makes *you* my aunt."

Milly's eyes widened and she blinked several times. Then, she burst out into giggles.

"That's so cool! Say hi to Harrie for me. I mean, your *mum*." She giggled again.

As we walked out of the control room, there were about a million things I wanted to ask, like why she never got any older ... and how she'd survived in here ... and if Mum ever did anything crazy like sneak out of the house in the middle of the night. But I was distracted by the sight of Emma, fifteen metres in the air, scaling the scaffolding of the big top. My jaw dropped in shock. I'd be less surprised to see Lucas in a weightlifting competition or Keira in a cupcake bake-a-thon.

"Hey!" I yelled. "What are you doing up there?"

Emma untangled a huge rope from the top. She flung it over her shoulder, shinned down the side and jumped to the ground. She wiped the sweat from her forehead, shaking a little, but smiling widely.

"Not so scared of heights any more?" I said.

"After that roller coaster," she said, "I don't think anything can scare me. Well, except your PE socks."

"Awesome," I said, laughing. "Hey! You're not going to believe this . . . " I turned around to grab Milly.

But she was gone.

"Believe what?" Emma said.

I shook my head. She'd been there a second ago . . . Was Milly just a ghost? Or a hallucination? What about the rest of the kids? Were they just . . . spirits?

"Um, never mind," I said. "Right now we've got to get Lucas and Keira out of that pit."

Emma raised the rope. "My thoughts exactly."

We ran back up on to the platform and looked down. Keira and Lucas had wound their arms and legs around what was left of the netting, and Lucas was starting to look a little green as he glanced at the sea below.

"About time!" Keira yelled when she saw us. "Were you planning to wait until we were skeletons, too?"

"Funny," I said, then tossed the end of the rope down to them. Keira and Lucas reached for it. "Come on! Let's get out of here!"

As Lucas and Keira heaved themselves up the rope I peered into the pit. There was no sign of Happy's crazed orange hair anywhere in the sea below. The clown was gone. For good.

Lucas and Keira reached the top and scrambled over the edge, shaking balls from their clothes. A small bone stuck from Lucas's ratty hair. Emma plucked it out and chucked it back into the pit, grimacing.

"I'm just gonna pretend that was plastic," she muttered.

"How do we get out of this place?" Keira said.

No way was I going back through that hall of mirrors. There had to be another way out. I searched the tent, and spotted a flap on the opposite side from the control room. I pointed at it.

"I don't know," Lucas said. "It's not a 'fire exit', is it?"

I shrugged. "Let's hope not. Only one way to find out."

We bolted over to it. I took a deep breath and carefully pulled it open. Immediately we were smacked in the face by ... warm, salt air.

"Yes!" Keira said.

We ran back out on to the pier and raced through the theme park, winding down the pathways until finally, huffing and puffing, we reached the open gates. The Happy statue's arm continued to creak up and down. Up and down. Lucas walked over and kicked the thing in the shin.

"Owwww!" he said, rubbing his foot.

Emma, Keira and I laughed. "Let's go, tough guy," I said. "Together."

The four of us headed towards the exit.

But before we could make it past the gate, a horde of rats swarmed over our feet. More rats than we'd seen all night. Keira screamed and stomped her boots.

"Not again!" she yelled.

But the rats kept coming. And coming. They formed a squirming wall across the turnstiles, completely blocking our path. Their beady red eyes flashed in the moonlight.

"What's going on?" Lucas said.

"I'll tell you what's going on!" A figure darted out from behind the dilapidated statue. My heart sank.

It was Happy the Clown.

If he'd looked freaky before, now he was a thousand times worse. The smile was completely wiped from his face. His blood red mouth was twisted into a horrible scowl of fury. Even his black eye make-up was little more than a thin line of hate.

"What's going on?" he sneered. "You four are not going anywhere!"

"Oh, no, no, no, no, no!" Lucas said, putting his face in his hands.

Happy adjusted his damp clown outfit, picking seaweed from his sleeve. "You didn't think it would be that easy, did you? That you could just release all my happy little helpers and not pay the price? Now you'll have to run the park. All by yourselves. For ever!"

He pursed his lips and drew in a breath to whistle. But before he could command his rats, I popped two

fingers in my mouth and let out my own high-pitched whistle – using just the same tones the robot Happy used in the Ghost Train.

Happy grimaced and whistled harder. I did the same. Emma, Keira and Lucas slapped their hands over their ears. The rats ran forward and backward, confused. I started to run out of breath. I didn't know how long I could keep this up. A satisfied smirk crept over Happy's face.

No way, I thought. *No way am I letting you win!*

I closed my eyes and pictured Milly. And Mum. And my friends and all the kids Happy had stolen. I sucked in one massive breath and blew as hard as I could.

My whistle could have cracked steel.

The rats froze in their tracks.

Then all at once they turned tail and swarmed

towards Happy. He tried to whistle, but no sound came out. The first of the rats covered his feet.

"Get off me!" he yelled. He tried to kick them off, but there were too many. They climbed over each other, squirming up his shins to his knees.

"It's not funny any more!" He thrashed his arms and legs. The rats kept climbing, gnawing his sleeves, scampering up his neck and over his face, their claws tangling in his hair. All I could see was a pair of shocked red eyes staring back at us in fear.

"Noooooooo!" Happy screamed as he toppled over and hit the boards. He screeched in pain as his jerking limbs disappeared completely under a sea of tails and fur and chattering teeth. "You haven't seen the last of me!"

But all we could see was a tuft of Happy's orange hair as the rats whisked him away.

CHAPTER 14

"That was some birthday party, Toby," Emma said as we made our way back home. She held her phone in the air, reviewing the night's footage.

"Sure was," Lucas said, nudging my arm. "And we've even got party hats!" He pulled the colourful paper cone from his head and inspected it. "Maybe this could be my new lucky hat ... Then again, maybe not."

We laughed as he crumpled the thing and chucked it in a nearby rubbish bin.

The sun was just beginning to creep over the horizon. Random lights flicked on in the houses along the road. Cats darted between bushes. Every now and then the sound of a car engine broke the silence. I was exhausted, but started to walk faster. Mum and Dad would be up any minute now. I really didn't want to have to explain what I'd been doing all night. I wasn't even sure I could.

Finally, we reached the end of my street. Keira shuffled to a stop.

"I'm over that way," she said, jabbing her thumb over her shoulder.

"OK, see you then." I turned up my road and kept walking. But Keira didn't move.

"Hey, hold up!" she said.

Lucas, Emma and I stopped. Keira kicked a few loose pebbles with her scuffed-up boot. Emma raised an eyebrow.

"Look," Keira finally said. "Maybe I was wrong about you three. Maybe you're not *complete* losers." She kicked more pebbles. Lucas instinctively dodged to the side. "Maybe you're actually OK," she said and shrugged.

Emma, Lucas and I looked at each other. "Maybe you're not so bad yourself," I said. I walked back to her and stuck my hand out. Keira smiled and placed her hand on top. Emma and Lucas nodded and added their hands to the pile.

We shook our hands three times and lifted them high over our heads.

"See you at school next week," Keira said. She turned and walked in the other direction. Lucas, Emma and I stared after her.

"Wow. Never thought I'd see the day ..." Emma said.

"See what day?" I asked. "The day that we'd get tickets to an abandoned amusement park, survive deadly rides and battle a psycho clown?"

"Uh, no," Emma said. "The day that Keira Ramone would actually be *nice*."

Lucas and I cracked up. We turned and walked along the road towards my house.

"What was it you said, Toby?" Lucas asked. "They don't call this place Weirdsville for nothing!"

That did it. We doubled over laughing. We were nearly in tears when we reached the gate to my house.

"Hey, Toby," Emma said, stopping. "We never did find your ball."

I looked at my house, porch light still lit, flowers covered in early morning dew. I closed my eyes and took a deep breath. I'd never seen a sweeter sight. Home.

"You know, it's OK," I said. "There are more important things in life."

I reached over and grabbed Lucas and Emma by the arms.

"Shhh," I said. "If we're quiet, maybe we can sneak back in without waking anyone."

We crept through the gate, down the path and up the porch steps. Every creak of wood beneath our feet seemed as loud as a firework. I slowly reached for the front door.

But before I could touch it, the door flew open.

"Aaagh!" we screamed in unison, jumping backward.

Mum stood on the other side, in her nightdress, a glass of water in her hand, wild-eyed, hair nearly as crazy as Happy the Clown's. Oh, man. Nothing good could come of this. It was bad enough getting caught sneaking out. Clearly, we'd also managed to disturb Mum's "beauty sleep".

"What on earth is going on?" She wagged a finger at us. "Where have you been? I woke up, went for some water and saw your bedroom door open. I've been worried sick! Don't you know not to run off at all hours? I'd think at your age you'd know better . . . "

My heart sank as she hurled accusation after accusation. "I'm sorry, Mum, really," I broke in. "If you'd just let me explain." I scrambled to find the words. "You see, this afternoon when we were playing—"

Mum cut me off by raising an eyebrow.

"We, um . . . "

"Ouch!" Lucas yelled. I looked at my best friend. He was rubbing his right calf and searching the porch floor. "What was that?"

The answer rolled to a stop behind us in the grass.

My ball.

My brand new, Nike T90 hand-stitched football.

Emma, Lucas and I stared at each other, eyes wide.

"Well," Mum said. "You were about to explain?" She tapped her slipper.

I began to open my mouth, but a familiar voice interrupted from the end of the driveway.

"I think that ball belongs to you!" Suddenly, all the colour drained from Mum's face. The glass of water slipped from her fingers and smashed. She lifted a shaking hand to her cheek.

I spun around to see someone leaning over the gate. Milly grinned and waved.

Mum gripped the door frame, blinking rapidly. "Camille?" she murmured. "But ... you ... " Then she fainted to the floor.

Milly bit her bottom lip. "Uh-oh," she said. "Didn't mean to do that . . . "

"I think you'd better come in," I said. "We're going to have a lot of explaining to do."